MEET ME IN MONTE CARLO

Sylvia leads a simple and ordinary life until her trip to Monte Carlo. How could she have imagined that things would change so suddenly and dramatically? That her love, Johnny, would leave her — only to reappear as a mystery man working with a gang of jewel thieves? That she'd dine and dance with one of the most dangerous criminals in France — and end up in a mad rush down the exotic Côte d'Azur with him? Will Sylvia and Johnny see their way through the danger and back to each other?

(r̶e̶g̶i̶s̶t̶e̶r̶e̶d̶ ̶c̶h̶a̶r̶i̶t̶y̶ ̶n̶u̶m̶b̶e̶r̶**)**
was established in 1972 to provide funds for
research, diagnosis and treatment of eye diseases.
Examples of major projects funded by
the Ulverscroft Foundation are:-

- The Children's Eye Unit at Moorfields Eye Hospital, London
- The Ulverscroft Children's Eye Unit at Great Ormond Street Hospital for Sick Children
- Funding research into eye diseases and treatment at the Department of Ophthalmology, University of Leicester
- The Ulverscroft Vision Research Group, Institute of Child Health
- Twin operating theatres at the Western Ophthalmic Hospital, London
- The Chair of Ophthalmology at the Royal Australian College of Ophthalmologists

You can help further the work of the Foundation
by making a donation or leaving a legacy.
Every contribution is gratefully received. If you
would like to help support the Foundation or
require further information, please contact:

THE ULVERSCROFT FOUNDATION
The Green, Bradgate Road, Anstey
Leicester LE7 7FU, England
Tel: (0116) 236 4325

website: www.ulverscroft-foundation.org.uk

DENISE ROBINS

◆

MEET ME IN MONTE CARLO

Complete and Unabridged

LINFORD
Leicester

First published in Great Britain in 1955

First Linford Edition
published 2020

A catalogue record for this book is available
from the British Library.

ISBN 978–1–4448–4528–0

Published by
Ulverscroft Limited
Anstey, Leicestershire

Set by Words & Graphics Ltd.
Anstey, Leicestershire
Printed and bound in Great Britain by
T. J. International Ltd., Padstow, Cornwall

This book is printed on acid-free paper

1

Until the time that Sylvia went to
Monte Carlo with her Australian
cousin, she had led a perfectly
ordinary, simple life. How was she to
dream that that life was to be so
suddenly and dramatically altered?
That Johnny, whom she loved, was to
leave her, then reappear as a 'mystery
man' working in with a gang of jewel
thieves? How was she to foresee that
her peaceful existence as she had
always known it would be exchanged
for a mad rush down the exotic *Côte
d'Azur* in the company of one of the
most dangerous and clever criminals
in France? That she was to dine with
him, dance with him, listen to him
talk, not knowing that he was a 'thief'
and even a 'killer'? That she was to
stroke the sleek coat of Setti, his
Alsatian, thinking the dog a harmless

1

pet and yet it, too, was trained to *kill*?

How could she foresee a day when she and Johnny would stand together before a shuttered villa behind Monte Carlo and hear the spatter of bullets breaking the silence of the drowsy golden afternoon, while the police tried to shoot their way through barred doors and sealed windows, and rout out the man with a price on his head?

None of these things seemed at all possible in the life of a girl like Sylvia Byrne, and yet they came to pass. And she was to live through those few staggering days of wildest excitement, drawn into playing a part in a strange, fast-moving drama of life, death — and of love.

No — none of this seemed possible to Sylvia when on a certain afternoon that first momentous telephone call came through to Broadcasting House and reached the office in which Sylvia worked.

She lifted the receiver and answered:

'Mr Fitzclair's secretary speaking . . . '

She supposed that she was about to have another of those boring conversations which droned on most of the day. It wasn't all 'fun and games' being personal assistant to a producer at Broadcasting House. Of course it had its exciting moments. She loved the big, vital building with its great halls and labyrinth of corridors, its little rooms marked 'Silence', the warning lights, the thousands of people hurrying to and fro, and the whole stupendous daily offering to the world of Talks, Music and general entertainment. She felt quite proud and patriotic every time she walked down Langham Place, passed through those imposing doors and realized that she, Sylvia Byrne, had become a cog, if only a very little one, in the machinery that flashed those messages from one end of the world to the other. And she liked her chief, Mr Fitzclair, who was a clever young man and just a little teeny-weeny bit in love with her. Yesterday when she was taking a letter for him he had suddenly said:

'You know, Sylvia, you're just like the Tanagra figurine that stands on my grandmother's mantelpiece. Such a diminutive little figure, and with that blonde hair curling to the nape of your neck like a baby's and your big eyes — you've got 'something' for me!'

She had laughed it off and managed to steer his thoughts back into the channels of work. She didn't want to 'have anything' for Aubrey Fitzclair, neither did she mind whether she resembled his grandmother's Tanagra figurine or not. She had got this job with a bit of influence and was glad to have it, but only with the intention of working furiously eight hours a day in order to take her mind off Johnny.

It didn't seem much use thinking too frequently about Johnny. But she was quite hopelessly in love with him. It hurt being in love with a man who is thousands of miles away in Korea, and who might at any moment be wounded or taken prisoner by those awful Communist Chinese or ... but she never allowed her thoughts to focus on the ultimate horror that might overtake Johnny and blot him out of existence. Neither would it be very easy to imagine Johnny being blotted out; the big, athletic fellow with his curly hair, his gay laughing face and those strong arms which could pick her up and carry her round the room as though she were a child. Six foot four was Johnny. Sylvia's fair head barely reached his shoulder.

Oh, but she loved him! And he loved her, too. Without being officially engaged, they had an understanding that, when he got back from doing his National Service, he would find a suitable job and then they could get married and live happily ever afterwards.

There was no reason why it shouldn't be so. They were both young and full of *joie de vivre*. Before Johnny had left England, Sylvia had been quite blissful.

It had seemed to her that they were two lucky people. Everything lay in front of them.

Sylvia's father was Principal Lecturer in Surgery at one of the biggest medical schools in London. She had an adored and adoring mother, and a beautiful home in Wimpole Street. Sylvia was working not because she needed the money but because she had an active mind and could not stay idle in the circumstances — while Johnny was away.

Johnny had been a medical student at Mr Byrne's hospital at the same time as Sylvia's cousin, Tom Byrne. Sylvia had gone to one of the dances there with Tom. But it was with Johnny that she danced most of the night. They had just tumbled into love with each other. He had said all the nice things that Aubrey Fitzclair said — and more. And she had thought that there wasn't a man in the world to compare with him either for charm, looks or humour. And one must marry a man with a sense of humour

— to that Sylvia had firmly made up her mind.

So Johnny Garland became the Chosen One for Sylvia, and the best thing of all was that her mother and father liked him. Daddy, in particular, said that young Garland was a sound fellow who ought to do well. As for Mummy — she had cherished the fond wish that lay in the heart of so many mothers that her darling would make a 'brilliant match'. There would be nothing 'brilliant' about marriage with Johnny, but she liked him immensely.

He hadn't a bean. He had lost his parents when he was a small boy — had no money coming to him; only a good education behind him and the small legacy from a fond aunt which had enabled him to take up medicine. Above all things, Johnny was a born doctor, and one of the first things Sylvia had admired was his finely made, sensitive fingers and his deep sympathy for suffering humanity which lay behind the façade of 'fun'.

If Sylvia had had her way she would have married Johnny before the Army swallowed him up and he left with the R.A.M.C. for the menacing shadow of the Korean campaign. But that he would not hear of. He wasn't the sort of young man to take advantage of the fact that Sylvia was the daughter of his chief; that he had a lot to gain by becoming Alec Byrne's son-in-law. On the contrary, Johnny was proud and it was a pride, so Sylvia discovered, that could at times be uncomfortably obdurate. He wanted to make his way first and *then* get married, he said. She had tried not to argue on the subject. She, too, had her pride. And if Johnny did not want to marry her now — well, that was *that*. But it hadn't been at all funny seeing him off, aware that she wasn't even engaged to him.

'You know that I love you and that I'll love you till I die,' he had said, when he had held and kissed her for the last time.

She had not been able to answer

because she had been crying, her face burrowed into the curve of his arm. He had kept hugging her and repeating:

'I do love you, Silver. You know that I do. Time will soon pass, and when I get back I'll find a damn' good hospital job and then put on a morning coat and silk hat, and approach your parents, carrying an expensive bouquet, and ask for your lily-white hand.'

He had laughed and she had laughed with him while the tears continued to drip forlornly down her small nose.

After he had gone she was not to be comforted. Her mother had been quite worried about her. And her father, who idolized her, openly declared that it was an infernal nuisance that little girls had to grow up and feel this way about big brutes of men.

Then Sylvia got her job at the B.B.C., set her teeth and put her heart into working as hard as she could. Every day she sent a letter to Johnny and he wrote back. Dear, comforting letters even if they were not particularly romantic. It wasn't quite Johnny Garland's line, writing poetic, amorous epistles. But he always ended with the only words that counted for Sylvia: '*I love you.*'

So the months dragged by and the Korean war went on and on and it was two years since she had seen Johnny. Now he was due home. Yet when his call came, Sylvia's thoughts were not particularly focused on Johnny. Why should they be, on this bleak January morning when she was trying to get through Mr Fitzclair's correspondence and having to keep breaking off in order to answer silly questions? What a nuisance budding script writers were, always wanting to know when their manuscripts were going to be read and if Mr Fitzclair had come to any decision.

'Hullo. This is Mr Fitzclair's secretary speaking,' Sylvia said again, as she had heard only a muffled bleat from the other end of the wire. And then, *then*, came that deep, rather lazy and wholly charming voice which she hadn't heard for two whole years.

'Is that by any chance Miss Sylvia Byrne?'

Sylvia turned positively pale. She clutched so violently at the gilt choker round her neck that it broke and crashed on to her typewriter.

'*Johnny!*' she gasped.

'Then it is you, Silver.'

She gulped. She tried to speak. No words came. She changed from white to wild rose. She heard a singing in her ears and felt a pounding of her heart. It was the most tremendously exciting episode of her whole life. *Silver.* His own particular name for her. He had given it to her on the very first night they had met at the Hospital Ball.

'*You little small blonde thing, you look as though you're made of silver,*' he had said.

'Hullo, hullo,' repeated the voice, and at this juncture, intercepting the call, came the familiar voice of one of the B.B.C. telephonists:

'Have you finished, Miss Byrne? There's someone waiting to speak to Mr Fitzclair.'

'No, I haven't finished. *Don't* cut me off,' said Sylvia wildly. 'Johnny, *Johnny!*'

'Hullo, yes, darling, I'm here.'

'Where?'

'Liverpool. Landed half an hour ago. There's a stream of us waiting outside the telephone-box so I can't stay long. But I'm catching a train straight away and I ought to be at Wimpole Street by dinner time.'

The tears gushed into her eyes. They were the happiest tears she had shed for twenty-four long, lonely months. They seemed to wash all the heartache and depression away.

'Oh, Johnny!' was all she could say.

'Angel — it's heaven to hear you. You sound sort of hoarse. Have you got a cold?'

'No, I haven't,' she sobbed, 'have you?'

'No. The grey docks of Liverpool look mighty good to me. Can't *tell* you what it's like to be back.'

'Are you really home for good?'

'For good.'

'Oh, I can't wait!' said Sylvia, and her hand shook so much that she nearly dropped the telephone.

'Tonight,' came Johnny's voice, 'and would you be an angel and let old Mrs What-not know at my digs that I'll be back? I did send her a line but she might not have got it.'

'I won't,' said Sylvia; 'you're going to stay with us, this week-end anyhow.'

'Just as obstinate as ever,' he laughed.

'Aren't you?'

'Just . . . '

'Oh, Johnny, I've missed you so. I can't *breathe*, I'm so excited.'

'Well, for heaven's sake don't stop breathing till I've seen you again, darling.'

Back came the intercepting, emotionless voice of the operator.

'Can you take this call for Mr Fitzclair, please, Miss Byrne?'

And after that it seemed that Sylvia

had no choice. The line from Liverpool faded away and with it Johnny. She had to control her agitation and take the call which was from just another luckless author wondering whether his script had been received or not.

A new and radiant Sylvia, in rapturous mood, gave him more hope than he deserved.

'Yes, I'm sure Mr Fitzclair will have read your MS. by now and you'll get a letter quite soon.'

Then she hung up. She sprang to her feet, stretched her arms above her head, and shut her eyes. So strong was her imagination that she could already feel Johnny's arms around her and his kisses on her mouth.

'*Johnny!*' she cried aloud.

A slim, dark-haired young man with a sheaf of papers in his hand walked into the office. A little coldly he looked at the figure of Miss Byrne with her upraised arms and her young, ecstatic face. The pretty, fine-boned face with its tip-tilted nose and entrancing eyes, and the petite figure outlined under the powder blue cashmere jersey and neat grey skirt had for some time now had a very disturbing effect on Mr Aubrey Fitzclair. He had been a little put out lately by the owner's obvious reluctance to accept his homage.

'Really, Miss Byrne!' he said, raising his eyebrows, and clicking his tongue.

'Oh, Mr Fitzclair,' exclaimed Sylvia, 'Johnny's come home.'

Mr Fitzclair's eyebrows remained raised.

'Johnny?'

'Yes, my fiancé.' (Sylvia was a little conscience-stricken after using this unauthentic title.)

'Oh, I see,' said Mr Fitzclair bleakly.

'He's been in Korea, you know, with the R.A.M.C. Now he's going to be a civilian doctor. He qualified before he was called up.'

'Good show,' said Mr Fitzclair in the same bleak voice. 'Do I take it that I am about to lose my secretary?'

'I'm afraid so,' said Sylvia.

Aubrey Fitzclair scowled and threw his papers on to the desk. To lose an efficient secretary who also had a most delightful figure must be termed a sad loss to any man.

'Don't look so pleased about it — you slay me,' he said darkly.

'Oh, I'm sorry, but I'm so happy!'

'Are you really so attached to this Johnny fellow?'

'Yes, I am.'

'Then we'd better call it a day. You are released. But give me a week in which to replace you, will you?'

'But of course, Mr Fitzclair. That goes without saying.'

He flung her a bitter look.

'You're a heartless young woman and you disappoint me. You don't seem to realize that you have administered a mortal blow to me.'

An intriguing dimple appeared at one corner of Sylvia's mouth.

'Oh, there are lots of girls better than I am, Mr Fitzclair. You'll soon find a good secretary.'

'Pardon me,' said Mr Fitzclair haughtily, 'if I fail to agree with you, and as I can barely endure your abominable look of smug satisfaction, I suggest, Miss Byrne, that you abandon the B.B.C. now, this moment, and go, oh, go to — *Johnny!*' he ended, tugging at his collar.

'Are you angry with me?' asked Sylvia timidly.

'No. Only damnably envious — of Johnny,' he said.

2

'He said that he envied you damnably, Johnny,' Sylvia recounted the story in her happiest voice to the object of her devotion.

They were sitting side by side on the big nole sofa in the Byrne's drawing-room on the first floor of the tall, dignified house which Mr Byrne, M.D., F.R.C.S., had occupied for the last fifteen years.

It was a very handsome room full of beautiful things. Old Markham, the Byrne's manservant, who had also been here since Sylvia was a small girl in the nursery, had just cleared away the coffee cups. Sylvia's parents had conveniently gone out to dinner. Johnny and Sylvia had dined alone. They had agreed that it would be much nicer to stay and eat here quietly by themselves, on this first night of the soldier's return.

Tomorrow, if they so desired, they could celebrate — go out to a meal and dance.

Johnny lit the cigar that Mr Byrne had left for him and took a sip of the Calvados which was Mr Byrne's favourite liqueur. It had a fiery warmth which made Johnny feel good — like the champagne which had also been left for the celebration. Everything had been good tonight after that hell, working day and night on pitifully wounded men. After all the carnage, the bestiality of war, it seemed exquisitely peaceful in this lovely London house; wonderful to wear a civilian suit again instead of uniform; to eat a *recherché* and civilized meal. And above all to be with Sylvia. A more appealing, fragile-looking and yet vital girl he had never known. He had kept the image of her in his heart for two long years and never wavered in his fealty, or his desire to return to her. There had been a lot of girl-friends in handsome Johnny Garland's life during his early years at the medical school. He had a peculiar charm for women. And he liked them, too. He wanted, in time, a wife, a home and children. In meeting Sylvia Byrne he knew that he had discovered his beau-ideal. So far so good. But all was not quite perfect. The fly in the ointment for Johnny was the fact that she was the daughter of a great man in the medical world, and a rich man at that, and that Johnny Garland was a penniless doctor. Johnny had strong principles. An unshakable conviction that man should be the breadwinner, and that until he was capable of supporting a wife, he should not marry.

He had thought it all over when he first fell in love with Sylvia. He had been thinking about it while he was away from her. He knew that he could not stop loving her. He knew, too, from her lovely letters that she had remained devoted to him. She was his for the asking. But he wasn't the man to take unless he could give, and for the moment he couldn't give Sylvia anything but love — all the love in the world certainly, but nothing else. He hadn't a penny. He would have to rely on getting a good hospital appointment in order to make a living. He might even have to go back into hospital for a while to 'freshen up'. He just wasn't in a position to get married. Yet Sylvia, during dinner, had let fall several remarks that led him to suppose that he *ought to marry her* now that he was back. Her father would find him a good job, she had said. He would use all his influence on Johnny's behalf. And he would make their marriage possible by giving Sylvia a good allowance. He could afford to. She was his 'ewe lamb'. There was absolutely no reason in Sylvia's mind why she should not take an impecunious physician, on the threshold of his career, for her husband.

But it didn't quite work that way with Johnny. He saw every reason to believe the reverse. He wasn't going to accept help from anybody, and the very thought of accepting financial aid from his wife or her parents was anathema to him.

So far this evening he had neither the heart nor the inclination to voice these feelings. He wanted to enjoy the glorious happiness of being with Sylvia again. They were so entirely in sympathy over most things. The little things that counted. The shared taste in books, in music, in all kinds of entertainment. They had the same sense of humour. And with it all that strong physical attraction that made them tremble when they touched each other's hands. He took many a covert look at Sylvia now as he drew in the aroma of his cigar, long legs stretched out before him. His tanned face bore an expression of deep satisfaction. How sweet she looked, his Silver girl. That exquisitely white skin looked transparent against the black velvet of her charming cocktail dress. Around the slender throat was a turquoise choker which seemed no bluer than her eyes. Her hair was cut shorter than it used to be. He liked the way it curled behind her small ears and fell into a deep crisp wave over the forehead. Her waist looked devastatingly small and attractive, a wide-silver-studded belt enclasping it. He murmured:

'My beloved Silver-girl. You know I used to dream about moments like this when I was out *there*.'

'And I used to dream a lot about you, too, Johnny.'

'Sure you didn't fall for your Mr Fitzclair?'

'Ask him,' she laughed. 'Didn't I just tell you that he made lots of passes at me and got no response? That's why he envied you.'

'Has he got any money?'

'I believe so.'

'Then *I* envy *him*.'

'Oh, Johnny!'

For the first time since she had heard his voice on the telephone telling her that he was home, her face clouded. Her heart was touched as though by a chill finger. She knew that tone in Johnny's voice and that sudden sombre expression darkening his sun-burned face. She knew him all too well. It was a 'thing' with Johnny — this having no money and being in what he called 'a lower strata of society' than herself. Useless to keep telling him that Daddy was once a poor student, and that Mummy had married him long before he became a specialist. Useless to bring up cases of other young couples who got married on nothing and were quite happy. Always in the old days, Johnny used to argue:

'There may be exceptions to the rule, but I think that no chap has the right to tie a girl like you down unless he can give her the sort of life to which she is accustomed. Besides, I am not the type to accept financial support from my wife, even if she is as sweet and lovely about it as you would be.'

She had so hoped that the two years in the Army might change his outlook and make him a trifle less conservative.

She had, perhaps foolishly, staked a lot on this change of mind. But now here he was, envying Aubrey Fitzclair his income; which meant only one thing — Johnny was still worrying about money. He hadn't lost that horrid chip on his shoulder.

Sylvia tried desperately to swing the conversation out of the dangerous channel. With somewhat forced gaiety she said:

'Well, I don't think *you* need envy *any* man. My Johnny has got the world in front of him. Dr Garland is going to be the great physician of the future. When Daddy's a tottering old man he will come and ask your opinion.'

Johnny laughed.

'What a hope!'

Sylvia laced her fingers around a crossed knee and looked at him through her lashes. They were thick and luxuriant lashes which Johnny found disturbing. To hell with money and principles. This was his first night back from Korea and he was alone with

Sylvia and they were in love. So what?

He laid his half-smoked cigar in an ashtray, turned to the girl beside him and pulled her against his heart. With one of his hands he smoothed back the gleaming silver-gilt hair. He looked at her with all the assurance of passionate love that she needed.

'Oh, my darling, my *darling*!' he said.

'Darling,' she repeated the word.

Their lips met. For a moment they kissed urgently, demandingly, love-hungry, desperately in need of each other. For those few moments Sylvia's generous heart was satisfied. She pressed her cheek to his and said again and again:

'I love you. Don't let me go. Keep me with you now that you're back, Johnny. Take me with you wherever you go.'

'Darling, you're sweet, much too sweet,' he said, and suddenly, gently but firmly, held her away from him and got up, straightening his tie and his ruffled hair.

She looked up at his face and saw

that it was pale and set. Her spirits ebbed again.

'Oh, Johnny, what is it?' she whispered.

'Don't ask me tonight,' he said, 'there's so much to be thought out and discussed. Don't let's make any important decisions now. Let's just be happy together.'

She knew then what lay in his mind. She sat very still. Her lips, still warm from his kisses, trembled. All the old fears returned to annihilate her happiness. Johnny had come back to her again. He was safe from the threat of death in Korea. He was as much in love with her as ever. Of that there was no doubt. But she knew perfectly well that he was just the same old implacable Johnny, and that no matter how much he wanted it, he would not be talked into an immediate marriage.

With a twist of the lips she sprang up from the sofa, walked to the radio-gramophone and deliberately switched it on to a foreign station from which there issued gay music.

'What about a dance?' she said with a toss of that silver-gilt head which Johnny found so attractive. He eyed her covertly. Sometimes a chap found it hard to understand the workings of a girl's mind. He knew enough about Sylvia to be sure that she was not quite happy about this situation, yet she seemed to be facing facts like himself. She wasn't making demands. That made him feel both ashamed and pleased. Yet why should he be ashamed of refusing to 'marry money'?

Now he took what the gods offered. He danced with Sylvia — having helped her roll back the rugs. He held her very close and she shut her eyes. They were cheek to cheek. She was warm and sweet and fragrant and this, for Johnny, was paradise after Korea. Neither of them spoke; perhaps neither of them dared, neither did they wish to spoil these lovely moments.

At eleven o'clock they were still dancing. The great surgeon walked in with his wife just in time to see his daughter executing a very neat Samba with her tall young doctor — looking as though she hadn't a care in the world.

Alec Byrne, small, thin, with greying hair and horn-rimmed glasses, put the evening paper he was carrying under his arm and applauded.

'Nice work,' he said.

Breathless and flushed, Sylvia giggled a little as she faced her parents. Johnny straightened his hair and tie.

'Hope we haven't made a mess of your lovely drawing-room, Mrs Byrne,' he addressed Sylvia's mother.

Mrs Byrne, who had once been as pretty and blonde as her daughter and was now on the plump side, assured him that it didn't matter. She was a great favourite with Johnny, was Sylvia's mother. He liked her beautifully-blued hair and the dimples that she had bequeathed to Sylvia. He liked the fact that she enjoyed her food and made no attempt to 'slim', and looked every inch her forty-eight years, if not more.

The four of them had drinks and gossiped until midnight. Then Mrs Byrne yawned and said that it was time for bed. Sylvia followed her. Not being officially engaged, she and Johnny made no attempt to kiss or touch hands in front of her parents. But they looked at each other and it was a look that hurt the girl profoundly. Johnny had fine bright eyes. They expressed a great deal of love in this instant; love that she needed; that she had hungered for. Yet the barrier was still up. The bridge of his pride and his determination which he would not cross in order to reach her wholly.

Mrs Byrne was quick to notice a complete change in Sylvia's expression and demeanour once they were upstairs. Sylvia had followed her mother into her bedroom and begun to take off her ear-rings. Mrs Byrne said:

'Enjoyed your evening, darling? It must be wonderful for you, having Johnny home.'

Then a rather white, tight-lipped girl swung round and faced her mother, a suspicion of tears glittering in her eyes.

'Yes, Mummy, but — '

'What, darling?'

'He just won't ask me to marry him,' said Sylvia in a suffocated voice, and swallowed hard.

Mrs Byrne looked grave. She couldn't bear Sylvia to be unhappy. She said:

'Why?'

'He's in love with me, but he says he has no job yet and he'll have to work so hard for a year or two until he can ask a girl to marry him.'

Mrs Byrne sat at her dressing-table and began to remove her own jewellery. The pain in Sylvia's eyes and voice hurt her.

'Well, darling, that's better than if he'd been the sort of boy to leap at the daughter of people who are more or less well off — not that any of us can call ourselves rich these days,' she added.

'It may be very worthy of him and all

that,' Sylvia burst out, 'but it's rotten for me. He's sacrificing himself as well. Just imagine having to wait two whole years!'

'But if Daddy can help — '

'He wouldn't let Daddy help financially,' broke in Sylvia; 'he wouldn't let Daddy do anything except recommend him for a decent appointment, perhaps, at the old hospital. Johnny does not approve of poor men having wives with means. He says it's got to be all equal.'

'Dear me,' murmured Mrs Byrne, 'Johnny's a little bit difficult.'

Then Sylvia put the back of her hand over her eyes and said in a choked voice:

'He is, and I love him. I love him so much, Mummy, I don't know what I am going to do.'

Mrs Byrne did not immediately get up and go to Sylvia and embrace her. She knew better than that. She knew Sylvia's soft heart and sensitive nature; too sensitive at times, perhaps. Better to let her try and harden up and face life, poor pet. It could be so implacable at times, thought the older woman with a sigh. No matter how much one tried to protect one's children, one could not altogether spare them. They had to face the music sooner or later. Johnny was being a trifle over-quixotic, perhaps, but at least it proved he was a decent man with fine feelings. But it was easy to understand Sylvia's feelings, too. Youth is impatient. Two years can seem so long to the young; so short to the old. And Johnny was a devastatingly handsome and attractive boy. It would be hard for Sylvia to watch him being swallowed up by his hospital life.

The mother said gently:

'Don't be too depressed, sweetie. Things work out and I dare say a solution will turn up.'

'I dare say,' said Sylvia darkly without conviction.

'Incidentally,' said Mrs Byrne, changing the conversation, 'just before I went out I opened that letter you gave me with the Australian stamp.'

Sylvia stood silent, brooding over her personal griefs whilst her mother told her what the letter from Lilian Byrne, her sister-in-law in Sydney, contained. Sylvia's cousin, Kay, who was a year or two older and a good deal more sophisticated and travelled, for she had had many jobs and led an independent life, was coming over to Europe in April or May.

'I remember seeing Kay as a child — a jolly good-looking little thing, and now Lil says she is nearly six foot, a bit mad but very nice and attractive. We'll have her to stay with us, shall we? It would be nice for you.'

Sylvia bit her lip. Nice for her to have a girl cousin from Australia to stay, when all she wanted was Johnny!

Sylvia felt suddenly that her cup of bitterness was full to overflowing. She wanted to be alone. She bade her mother good night and walked quickly into her own room. The great day was over. Johnny had come back. And Johnny didn't seem to be as much hers as while he was all those thousands of miles away in Korea.

She flung herself down on her bed and began to cry.

3

The next four or five months in Sylvia's life seemed the most difficult and on the whole the most miserable she had ever known. She swung from hope to despair and then back again, and the pendulum existence got on her nerves and made a very different Sylvia out of her. A Sylvia who lost most of her natural gaiety and would hardly have been recognized by her one-time employer at Broadcasting House. That Sylvia could always be relied upon to make a pert answer. This one had little spirit and was growing much too thin in the eyes of her fond parents.

Of course, Johnny was to blame. Yet how could they blame him? A man must live up to his principles. And he was not to be moved. He saw a great deal of Sylvia but discussion on their future was avoided. They were companions — they were, at moments, lovers. For them both it was a difficult period in which they would cling together in silent longing for the seemingly impossible. The nervous strain could not, of course, go on; one of them was bound to crack.

Johnny had accepted Mr Byrne's help in getting him on to the staff of one of the biggest hospitals in London. After which he became an internee. Work was intensive and the hours long. The great hospital was packed, and at the end of such days as those Johnny spent in seeing Out-Patients left him little time or energy for any kind of entertainment. Sometimes it was an effort to change and get along to Wimpole Street and take Sylvia out. Under the weight of work and responsibility he felt some of his own high spirits ebbing, and he, too, lost weight. But he adored his work. He was first and foremost a physician, and he wanted to 'make good'. And having a gay time, running round with a girl-friend, just didn't seem practical at the moment, even though the girl-friend was as dear to him as Sylvia. When he was with her he was enchanted by her — deeply in love. And he felt humble because she loved him so much; he felt unworthy. He was anxious to give her the world — do anything, in fact, except ask her to make an impecunious marriage.

If only she would wait . . .

At times Sylvia felt that she could and would wait, but at others she found the position unbearable. The day came when Johnny told her that he was getting a fortnight's break because the powers-that-be had transferred him to a new job as house physician in one of the biggest infirmaries in the Midlands, near Manchester.

Manchester! Sylvia repeated the word with a sinking heart.

They were sitting in the Park, facing the glittering Serpentine, in a small car which Sylvia had borrowed from her mother. It was a glorious evening late in May. The day had been warm and there was that magic touch of summer in the air which was both delightful and nostalgic. Johnny had been holding Sylvia's hand and was being particularly nice to her. She had been feeling a little less strained and unhappy. Then *this*. Sylvia's fingers tightened around Johnny's big fists until the points of her nails almost dug into his flesh.

'Manchester is a very long way,' she said in a small voice.

'Yes, but's a hell of a good job for me, darling, and it will lead to things. Your father himself said that it was experience that I needed and more responsibility which I also need.'

'I see.'

Sylvia was wearing sun-glasses. Through the darkened lens she looked not at Johnny but at some children feeding ducks on the water's edge. She thought what a long way Johnny would be from London. She wouldn't see him at all. This, then, was the end of her love dream.

'Darling, aren't you glad for me?' came his voice.

Suddenly she tore her fingers away from his.

'You're just a beastly egotist!' she said.

His face flushed.

'Well, I don't quite see that. After all, why do I want the job? To get on and make my way for you.'

Then she turned to him, her lips trembling, her eyes full of tears.

'Oh, Johnny, I know, but I can't *bear* such a long separation. I shall never see you. You'll always be too busy.'

'Oh, darling,' he said, 'it isn't going to be any better for me than for you. Anybody would think to hear you talk that I didn't *want* to marry you.'

'Sometimes I wonder if you do,' she flashed, and choked back her tears.

He folded his arms.

'I'm not going to argue about that. You know the truth.'

'And I'm not going to sit down in London and wait while you work up in Manchester, and there'll be lots of pretty probationers around you, and — and — ' she broke off and hid her face in her hands, terrified that she was going to burst into sobs then and there in the Park.

He slid an arm around her. He was as miserable as she was. So much so that he almost broke down and turned his back on his high ideals and asked her to go up to Manchester as his wife. But he had a swift picture of her leading an uncomfortable existence in gloomy, horrid rooms — nothing like her own beautiful home. What would be the good of such a life to his Sylvia? How could it be called fair to drag her into it? She would have the chance down here of meeting other men with much more money and in higher positions. Apart from which, how could he do justice to his new post and give a wife the attention she deserved? He was about to open his

mouth and say something to comfort
Sylvia when she suddenly flung back
her head and made a remark that
turned him cold.

'This ends it,' she said. 'If you're
going on being so stubborn and silly
— I'm through.'

Johnny went red.

'There you go — like all women, you
refuse to understand how a man feels.
You'd rather I was the sort of fellow
who'd think it smart to marry the
daughter of a famous surgeon and
feather his own nest.'

Sylvia set her teeth. She switched on
the engine.

'I'm going home,' she said.

Now Johnny's own temper flared up.
He flung her a bitter look.

'I'm getting fed up with your attitude
toward my job and my life,' he said.

It was her turn to flush scarlet.

'*You* are fed up! What about *me*?'

'Must we have a scene?'

'Not here. I'm going home.'

'Then you can drop me off, because I

don't want a scene here or anywhere else. I'm tired.'

She gasped.

'Johnny, are you trying to tell me that this is the end — of us?'

'I think it might be better, don't you?' he said in a cold voice.

She gasped again. She felt as though he had drained the Serpentine and flung the whole avalanche of water over her — drowned her — put an end to her whole life.

'Johnny!' she said in a horrified voice.

Two little white lines appeared on either side of his firm young mouth.

'Well — don't you think it would be better? We don't seem to see eye to eye these days. I love you but I'm *not* going to marry you till I've made my way. I think I'm right. You think I'm wrong. It isn't much good carrying on in these circumstances.'

'And I,' said Sylvia, 'don't believe that you love me at all.'

He opened his mouth as though to refute this, then shut it. He was indeed tired. He had had a heavy week and very little sleep, and he couldn't think straight. He only knew that his beloved Silver was showing herself as a self-centred, unsympathetic, difficult young woman. He got out of the car, lifted his hat and gave her a stiff bow.

'Forgive me if I take a walk. I need the fresh air. Thank you for — every-thing. Good-bye.'

She did not answer. She felt as though the blood was freezing in her veins. Inwardly, a terrified voice was calling: '*Johnny!*' But no sound came. She took off her sun-glasses and stared horrified at the sight of the tall, attractive figure walking away from her. It was the end, she thought wildly, the *absolute* end this time.

Then with trembling fingers she replaced her glasses, backed the car away from the water, and drove home.

As she parked the car outside her father's house, a taxi rolled up. A tall, dark girl with merry eyes and carrying a suitcase in each hand stepped out. They met face to face. The tall girl dropped the suitcases and with the suspicion of a twang, said:

'Ow — I'm *sure* I recognize you from your photos. You're my cousin Sylvia, aren't you? I'm Kay.'

'How do you do, Cousin Kay,' said Sylvia in a bleak little voice.

And it was that small, plaintive voice and the glint of tears in the loveliest of long-lashed eyes that made the big-hearted girl from Sydney take her English cousin right to her heart there and then. It wasn't until later that she learned just *why* Sylvia looked so unhappy, or heard all about the quarrel with Johnny. But it was a moment that marked the beginning of a strong affection and friendship between the two girls. An alliance that began in Wimpole Street and continued a fortnight later — in Monte Carlo.

4

Less than forty-eight hours after Kay's
arrival in London the Australian girl
was off again, this time with Sylvia as
her travelling companion.

They were flung into the glorious,
gay pandemonium of a mid-season
crossing from Newhaven to Dieppe.
The sea was like rippling blue silk in
the June sunshine. The crowd was
good-natured, jostling, packed like
sardines on the new French boat,
Lisieux.

Segregated in her misery, Sylvia
Byrne wish that a storm would blow up
and sink the beautiful new steamer,
taking her with it.

Everything had happened so quickly.
Kay seemed to have arrived at the
psychological moment. On the night
following her misunderstanding with
Johnny, she had hoped that he would

ring up and say that he had changed his mind. But he didn't. And from Mrs Byrne had come the advice:

'Don't whatever you do pursue him, darling. He'll come back.'

And from Sylvia:

'I don't care if he doesn't ... ' Strictly untrue.

From Mr Byrne:

'I suggest you get right out of England and have a fortnight in France now that you've got Kay to look after you. I'll give you each twenty-five pounds. No moping in luxury hotels, my poppet. You can take the train to Paris and then walk. Nothing like walking to cure depression; plus sunshine, new places, new faces. Get yourselves down to Monte Carlo. You'll be surprised how much better you'll soon feel.'

Kay had agreed. She bounded with health and good spirits. The tall, handsome young brunette was practical and amusing, and just the sort to help Sylvia to 'get over' Johnny.

Sylvia sat in her deck chair, feet on her rucksack, light, fleecy, pale blue coat folded over her knees, and knew she would never 'get over' him. Behind her dark glasses her large soft eyes, limpid as that summer sea, were blind with tears. She shut them rather than see the coastline fade from sight and remember that she was leaving behind her in England all that she loved most on earth.

She hardly heard Kay's cheerful voice as, with map on her knee, she began to trace out the route they would take. How they would thumb lifts from place to place; take picnics — long crisp 'flute' loaves and local *jambon* and cheeses and the *vin du pays*, and eventually taste the delights of a lazy sun-drenched life on the *Côte d'Azur*.

All that she could think about was how awful it was that Johnny hadn't rung up. It must, of course, mean that he hadn't loved her after all. For a ghastly moment she had even wondered if there wasn't another girl in his life.

48

There he was with a fortnight's holiday in front of him back in his digs, and what was he going to do? She didn't know, she might never know. She might never see him again.

Kay, who did a lot of talking, had offered a lot of sound advice, and like Mummy had told her to stop thinking about Johnny. But that was easier said than done.

Kay, cheerfully unwrapping a large slab of chocolate, broke off a piece and offered it to her cousin.

'I couldn't. I'd be sick,' she said.

'You haven't eaten a thing since I arrived in England, and you must try to get on top of this Johnny-thing,' said Kay.

Said Sylvia, 'I'd rather smoke.'

'Then have one of mine,' said a voice at her side.

Sylvia turned with a 'Thank you.'

'I'll go and get our quota,' said Kay, jumping up. 'They're cheaper on board.'

Sylvia took the cigarette she had been

offered. Through the dark glasses and the tears she saw a well-dressed young man with smooth fair hair, holding an open case out to her. She didn't like his thin, foxy face or the way he looked at her. But after the preliminary exchange of pleasantries about the good weather, he told her a story which put him in a new and more sympathetic light.

His name was Rex Harris. He owned a little antique shop in Chelsea. His adored wife, Pamela, had just died, and he was taking a holiday in France to try and forget her.

Another one trying to forget, thought Sylvia. And because she was so unhappy herself, she lost sight of the fact that she didn't like the young man's appearance, and tried to be nice and kind to him.

Then when Kay came back she told her about his tragedy, and before the boat reached Dieppe they were all the best of friends.

Kay, more perceptive than Sylvia, who was so easily guided by her emotions, whispered to her cousin:

'I think there's something queer about this Rex. I don't think I trust him, and we don't want him tacking on to us all the way — even if he is a bereaved widower.'

'Poor soul — we'll have to shed him in Paris,' Sylvia whispered back.

But they lunched together on board. Rex was particularly nice and attentive to Sylvia, who had mentioned that she, too, had loved and lost (though not by death), where-upon he further endeared himself to her by saying:

'It can, I know, be worse than death knowing that somebody you want is still in the world but you can't have them.'

She thought him most understanding. He carried her ruck-sack as they started to file with the crowd down the gang-way to the Customs shed. He looked at the back of the attractive, slimly-built girl in her dirndl skirt and loose yellow pullover, worn with a gay silk handkerchief knotted around her slender neck, and thought:

'Rather a smart little thing. I wouldn't mind consoling her.'

But he didn't think the big brunette would give him the chance, even if he could win the blonde over with a few more of those lovely lies about his fictitious wife. However, he had rather a lot on his mind and a few sticky moments ahead of him now at the Customs.

Kay looked at the attractive, sunlit little harbour, the narrow, shuttered houses still bearing the scars of war, and the familiar posters — *Cinzano, St Raphael*. This was *France*!

'Oh, what fun we're going to have!' she said ecstatically.

Sylvia thought:

'It might have been heaven if Johnny had come, too. *Why* did he walk out on me just because of Daddy's position? I bet he's as unhappy as I am right now. Oh, Johnny, you fool!'

Remembering the sorrowful Mr Harris, she turned to him and said: 'You were telling us you know Paris well. Perhaps you can recommend a good cheap hotel.'

He was about to answer when a man in uniform — a travel agent — waved a telegram at him and shouted: '*Monsieur Harris!*' Rex claimed the wire. The girls were too busy making their way to the Customs shed to notice that as he read it his face went a pale shade of green. He seemed to fall to pieces. It was quite a simple telegram:

'*Cream gone sour,*' it said.

It was, perhaps, odd, but that little message about the curdled cream distressed Mr Harris greatly. The girls moved on. Sylvia turned and called back at Rex:

'Hi! You've got my rucksack. Come on!'

'Coming!' he shouted back.

But he lost them for a moment in the crowd. Sweating profusely, he put his own case on the ground, lifted the lid and pulled out a tube of sun-proof cream — an innocent-looking pinkish tube. But he handled it as though it burnt his palm. His teeth clicked together. He mopped his brow, recovered himself and slipped the sun-proof cream into Sylvia's rucksack. Then he drew breath, felt better and joined the girls again. They all opened their bags, awaiting the chalk mark of authority, whilst outside the Paris-Nord express got up steam.

Sylvia looked around the Customs house. It had only recently been built and made an imposing feature of welcome for visitors. It was light, gay and sunny and Sylvia began to feel just a little better. After all, it gave one a warm feeling of agreeable anticipation. Here they were, actually in France, and France ought to be a lot of fun. The gentleman of the *douane*, smiling and unmenacing, strolled towards Sylvia and Kay and asked them, in French, if they had anything to declare — repeating the enquiry in broken English.

'Absolutely nothing,' Kay answered stoutly. 'What should a poor girl bring into France? The point is, what she is going to take out of it — *n'est-ce-pas?*'

And she smiled at her own sally, her flashing eyes responding to the Latin appreciation in the eyes of the man to whom she spoke. Sylvia added her little word:

'I know there is nothing in *my* rucksack that you'll worry about, but you can see if you like.'

And she began to unfasten the strap.

Behind her. Rex sweated blood. His face retained its greenish pallor. His heart pumped. He began to think that he wasn't much good at this sort of job and that he had better throw it up. The game wasn't worth the candle. If they found those emeralds — oh, *good night* — what then?

He hissed in Sylvia's ear:

'Nobody ever bothers about Customs over here — you don't have to turn out your things.'

'Pardon me,' said Sylvia haughtily. 'I've nothing to hide if he wants to take a look-see.'

And she dipped a slender hand into the rucksack.

Rex thought it best to totter on. If the worst happened and the tube of sun-proof cream was discovered — much better for him to be missing.

He began to walk away. He hardly dared look round and see what Sylvia was going to do next. But, fascinated, he had to throw a look over his shoulder. Then he breathed again and wiped his forehead. She was fastening the strap. The charming gentleman of the *douane* had placed his chalk mark upon the rucksack. Sylvia and Kay joined Rex, and they all three found themselves a corner each in the carriage of the Paris express. Sylvia curled up in a corner and tried to sleep, and to give herself up to her sad, romantic yearnings for Johnny. Kay dived into a detective novel.

Rex Harris kept an anxious gaze on Sylvia's rucksack. She had placed it in the rack above her head. He wondered what to do about that tube of sun-proof cream, and what Sylvia and Kay would say if they could squeeze it slowly out, plus the £20,000 worth of beautiful cut and polished emeralds which were mixed up with it.

5

The words of the telegram haunted Rex throughout the journey to Paris and continued to cause him a great deal of anxious thought. '*Cream gone sour!*' That meant someone had squealed. They were on his track. He had got through Dieppe all right. But they might be waiting for him at the Gare St Lazare. It wouldn't matter if they found nothing on him. Then it would be okay. They'd have to let him go and he could join the others in Dijon at the appointed place.

Kay glanced at him over her book.

'Hot, isn't it?'

'Too hot,' said Rex feelingly. He was perspiring. But it was with acute anxiety. He thought:

'I'd better leave the tube in Sylvia's rucksack for the moment. I'll get them to go to my hotel. Then later tonight I can ask Sylvia if I could borrow a tube of cream for sunburn. It'll be too easy. She may wonder how it got there, but think someone at home slipped it in at the last moment. Whatever happens *she must not use it first.*'

'You don't look well,' said Kay, and decided that not only did he look seedy but unpleasant. She didn't like him. She must get rid of the gloomy, fox-faced widower.

'I'm not very well,' said Rex suddenly, and thought of what Flick in London might do to him if he didn't get those emeralds back and deliver them to Henri Chausseur, the chief, at the old Château which had recently become a clearing house for the gang. The emeralds were from India and perfect. Once on the Continent it would be easy to sell them. But *sour cream* — damn it — that message from Flick meant someone had put the police on his trail. It just would happen when he, Rex, was doing his first big job. Flick had complimented him on the tube-of-cream-idea, too. It had been too easy taking off the head, filling the tube with the green gems, then sticking head and cap on again.

As the train steamed into the Gare St Lazare, Rex went into the corridor and Kay whispered to her cousin:

'Listen, Syl, we *must* shed Mr Harris. I can't stand him. I hate men who sweat so profusely!'

'I hate all men except Johnny,' said Sylvia, yawning.

Kay ignored this. She had been advised by her uncle to ignore any of Sylvia's feverish attacks until time and the holiday had taken effect. They decided to bid Mr Harris good-bye at the station and find themselves a little hotel.

But Rex stuck like a leech. Eagerly he recommended a *cute* little hotel near the *Madeleine*. The girls each in turn thanked him politely but assured him that they already had an hotel lined up.

'But Sylvia asked me to recommend

one . . . ' began Rex frantically. But this was where Miss Kay Byrne from Sydney asserted herself. She was a strong character. Once outside the station she hailed a taxi and bundled Sylvia into it. Rex, panting and feeling that he had made a fool of himself, made a grab at Sylvia.

'Hi! Wait! I — I was going to ask you — I got scorched on the boat — can you lend me some sun cream?' he stammered wildly.

'Don't be silly,' said Kay in an icy voice, and slammed the door in his face. She added to Sylvia: 'You speak French better than I do — tell the driver to go on — to the *Opera* — Cook's is there, according to my guide, and they'll find us a hotel. It's only for one night — we'll make an early start for Dijon tomorrow.'

Sylvia was about to reply, but paused, startled to see that Mr Rex Harris had jumped on to the footboard of the taxi. His face glared at her, livid and suddenly menacing.

61

'You've got to take me with you!' he shouted.

Suddenly Sylvia was scared of him, and shrank back.

'*Allons vite!* Get along — we don't want *monsieur* with us,' she said to the driver.

The taxi driver was young. He wore his beret at a rakish angle, and he thought the English *mademoiselle* as beautiful as an angel. His taxi shot forward. Mr Harris fell off the running-board and was at once surrounded by a sympathetic crowd.

When he regained his feet, bruised, shaken, and enraged, the taxi bearing his two charming companions of the channel crossing had gone. And £20,000 worth of emeralds with them!

He felt positively suicidal. Turning back into the station he found a telephone booth. There he put through a call to a certain flat in a big luxury block overlooking the Seine. He was much relieved when a woman's voice, speaking French, answered.

''Elo?'

'Oh, thank the stars you're in, Lucille,' he gasped.

The woman at the other end now spoke in tolerably good English.

'Ah! It is Rex?'

'Yes, it is, and I'm in the depths. I've had the most ghastly bit of bad luck.'

Her voice came sharply.

'You mean with the — ' she stopped significantly.

'Yes. I daren't speak about it on the phone. I must come straight to the flat and see you.'

'I was just about to go out. It is not convenient.'

'Lucille, you must *make* it so. You know what Henri is like. You *must* help.

The name of Henri and the pressing note in Rex's voice seemed to decide the woman Lucille.

'Oh, very well, come straight along,' she said irritably, 'but be queeck.'

Fuming and considerably depressed, Rex took a taxi to Lucille's flat. She was no ordinary girl-friend of the Chief's.

She was a very important person — both his mistress and confederate. When Henri was in Paris, it was with Lucille that he lived. When he wished it, she accompanied him to his country house. She had all the assets that a man like the Chief needed in the woman who shared his life; beauty, brains and daring. In addition Lucille had few scruples.

She received Rex in an exceedingly smart salon which was filled with flowers and redolent with a new Dior perfume. Lucille, herself in a Dior masterpiece, was strikingly handsome — dressed like a true French woman in faultless black. She had an exquisite little hat on her dark, close-cropped head. She smoked a cigarette in a long amber holder, and looked coldly through her blackened lashes at the crestfallen Rex. After listening to his story she gave a short laugh. Her nostrils quivered with disdain. '*Imbecile!*' she spat the French word at him.

'I did it for the best after reading that

telegram. Flick must know that the police are suspicious,' he gulped.

'It wasn't necessary for you to get ze cold feet and put the tube into a stranger's luggage,' Lucille snapped.

'I did it for the best,' he repeated.

'Then you had no right to lose sight of the girls.'

Rex jerked at his collar. The heat in Lucille's salon was overpowering. The burden of his own thoughts was weighty enough. He loathed this woman of Henri's. She was a vixen. She had glamour, yes, but she was a heartless vixen with her ice-cold brain and her passion for what money could buy. He said:

'I tell you the English girls vanished before I could follow them.'

Lucille's lips curled.

'Tell that to Henri.'

He flicked his lips. He wouldn't like to think what Henri would do to him; or Flick at the other end. Rex gave Lucille a dirty look. He would like to have thrown that slinky body of hers down on to the satin cushions on her own sofa and torn off her expensive clothes. Instead, he made a whining appeal.

'Help me, Lucille. You've got to. There's your big Citröen available, isn't there? Take me down to the South. The girls are hitch-hiking. They're going to Monte Carlo. We're bound to see them and pick them up *en route*.'

Lucille flicked the ash impatiently from her cigarette. She was well aware of the importance of this business. Particularly as Henri would be flung into the most atrocious mood once he got wind of Rex Harris's failure, and if Rex told him that she had refused him assistance, he would turn the guns on *her*. Yes, he would expect her to act and act swiftly in an emergency. It was more than *embêtant* from her point of view. She had a date this evening with a very charming young man. Of course, Henri didn't know anything about the said young man, but when Henri wasn't here — well — why should she be bored? And her boy-friend was a South American and danced divinely.

She could have kicked the English fool. She would tell Henri that it was time he gave instructions to throw Rex out. He was worse than useless to the gang. Now Rex was telling her excitedly about two men whom he had seen outside the telephone-booth at the station. Men wearing light raincoats and slouch hats. Scotland Yard had probably phoned through a description of him to the *Sûreté*. Rex walked to the window and peered down. He saw nobody. He wiped his face and repeated his appeal.

'I'll think it over,' said Lucille, flinging her cigarette-end into the grate.

'Damn it, you can't think — there's no time!' he grumbled.

She looked at her wrist-watch.

'I'm late now for an important appointment. Come down with me. I'll make up my mind as we go,' she said.

He was forced to follow her, raging and humiliated. They went down in the lift and out into the sunshine, where the Citröen and her chauffeur waited for her.

When she was seated, Rex began to repeat his whining appeal that she should help him. Then he saw her change colour.

'*Mon Dieu*,' she said softly, 'look behind you.'

He looked. And he saw two men approaching him. Two men wearing light raincoats and slouch hats. His breathing quickened. The sweat poured down his face. Through his teeth he said to Lucille:

'Now, perhaps, you'll believe me. They *are* following. It's the same two. *Now you'll have to go.* And you'll have to go alone because I expect they'll pick me up.'

'I could murder you,' said Lucille with an icy smile. 'No doubt Henri will do it for me. There's only one thing to hope for now and that is a cold, wet morning so that your English friends won't need sun-proof cream.'

'Find them,' said Rex in a hollow voice, 'and find them quick. That's my advice *to you*. I've given you a description of them. If the police search me they won't find a thing. They'll let me go and I'll follow you to Henri's.'

Lucille said a word in French which no true lady would have uttered. The chauffeur slipped in the clutch and the car moved away from the kerb.

The two gentlemen in raincoats closed in, one on either side of Rex.

On the following morning as dawn broke over the capital, Lucille in the big black Citröen was driven by her chauffeur through the suburbs towards the *Porte de Clignancourt*.

She was, as usual, as chic as a mannequin, but she had exchanged her black ensemble for a more sporting one in spotless white linen. With it she wore long gold ear-rings and three or four jangling gold bracelets. Her exquisitely painted face was dark as a thunder cloud. Now and again she snapped an order at the chauffeur, who touched his peaked cap and nodded silently. He was used to Mademoiselle Lucille's bad tempers. And she, who loathed getting up early, was thinking:

'*Diable!* Why did Flick give the emeralds to such an amateur?'

She had to cancel her date with the South American. Somewhere in Paris she presumed that the wretched English girls had spent the night, and quite soon would be starting on their stupid 'hike' down to Monte Carlo. It would have been impossible for Lucille to dance until the early hours of the morning, then get up at dawn to begin this journey. Not having heard another word from Rex, she could take it that he was being held for questioning despite the fact that he had nothing on him that could give rise to suspicion. Lucille had had a short cryptic conversation with Henri over the phone. He hadn't been very pleasant. He had said what she had expected; that she would not get another franc out of him until she found those girls

— and the emeralds!

On the bus, Sylvia and Kay, having had a good night's rest, were also on their way to *Clignancourt*. They were going to buy some food at an *epicerie*, then find somebody to give them a lift through Fontainebleau and Laroche. If they were lucky, they would make Dijon before nightfall. They had almost forgotten Rex Harris, although the soft-hearted Sylvia hoped that he hadn't hurt himself when he fell off the running-board at the station. Kay said that she hoped he had.

'I don't know what he was after; probably *you* — but I'd *had* it as far as he was concerned.

The morning was fresh and beautiful; the trees in the Boulevards an exquisite green. A golden journey lay before them, and they felt a long long way from England as they set out on the first stage of their journey. But Sylvia kept seeing Johnny's square young face and very blue eyes; and how awful it was to know they had parted in anger, unable to see each other's point of view.

'Oh, Kay,' she burst out, 'do you think Johnny was *right* not wanting to marry me now?'

'No, not if he really loved you,' said Kay. 'I don't think money should be made a stumbling block to love, any more than poverty.'

'Can't I send him a wire and tell him so?' asked Sylvia wistfully.

'Don't be silly, honey. Leave him alone. He'll come round to my way of thinking. You wait!'

Which, if Sylvia had but known it, was what Johnny Garland was doing at that precise moment. He had tried to be awfully determined and relieved that he had 'broken it off', and completely failed. Life without Sylvia was damnable. He had a night's heavy drinking and came out of an alcoholic daze vowing that he would remain sober for ever more, and that he could not possibly let Sylvia go out of his life. He had hurt her and himself through his damnable pride. It wasn't to be endured. When he had heard from Alec Byrne, himself, that Sylvia and her Australian cousin had gone off to the South of France, he knew that nothing else mattered except immediately getting in touch with her again. What the hell was life worth without Sylvia? And who was to know what might not happen to her on the glamorous *Côte d'Azur.*

He rang up his best friend, Bob Blunt. Bob was as rich as Johnny was poor. His father manufactured Blunt's famous commercial vans and made vast piles of dollars on the export side — besides which, Blunt's vans were to be seen all over Great Britain.

Johnny told Bob about the hospital appointment and the mistaken quarrel with his Sylvia.

'I've got a fortnight to play in before I start my job. I wish to God I could go down to the South of France and find her,' he said.

Bob's answer was crisp and brought a gleam of light into Johnny's darkness.

'And why not? I'm shipping six of Blunt's ruddy vans over the Continent tonight. It's too late for me to get my own car on the ferry, but we could drive one of the vans down to Monte if you like. Howse about it?'

'It sounds too good to be true,' said Johnny, 'but I can't — '

'Now listen, you old so-and-so,' interrupted Bob Blunt's cheerful voice, 'you're going to tell me you can't afford it and you won't let *me* pay. Listen. You're not too proud to *earn* some money, are you?'

'That's different.'

'Then I'll sign you on as a temporary employee of Blunt's Vans, Ltd, and you can take the consignment of vans over for me, and we'll use one of 'em, and be darned if I don't join you. You can do most of the driving and wash the darned thing down every evening while the boss drinks pernod in a café and finds himself a *jolie mademoiselle!*'

Bob ended with a guffaw of laughter. It was a laugh that made people raise their brows when they heard it in a public place, but in the end they had to smile because it was so infectious. Johnny had never known a nicer fellow than Bob. Success had never spoiled him. He had a quick vision of the man: six foot four, Johnny's own height, but massively built with a deep chest and long arms of a boxer. His hobby was amateur boxing.

Only another moment or two of conversation, and Johnny gave in. As a temporary employee of Blunt's he would take and deliver the vans to the manufacturing firm in Paris that had ordered them. Five of them could stay in dock and await the usual formalities, but one of them would be claimed by Johnny as his private automobile.

Bob finished:

'See you at Folkestone, Johnny. Make sure your passport's all right. I can't go with you but I'll fly over to Paris in the morning. Wait for me in the Ritz bar. I'll bring the cash. You can take the five you're allowed, and that's all you'll need till we meet. I'll register the van and get everything settled in my name. It'll be too easy! So long, old boy.'

'Wait — ' but Johnny got no further than that one word. There was silence. Typical of Bob. Mad as a hatter and quite delightful. But he always kept his word. He'd be there at the harbour tonight, all right, with the necessary papers for Johnny.

Johnny rushed home to his digs. He told his landlady he'd be away for two weeks, and threw a few clothes into a suitcase. As he jerked open the top drawer of his dressing-chest to find collars and ties, he paused and looked at a photograph of Sylvia on the mantelpiece. He ached with sudden longing for her. His Silver-girl with her wide, dreamy eyes and passionate young mouth.

'I was a mug to let my pride come between us,' he said remorsefully, and continued a wild search for a clean shirt and a pair of slacks with some sort of crease in them. What a thing to be a bachelor and have no one to look after you! There hadn't been anybody since his mother died. He was beginning to think it would be wonderful to have a wife — and that wife just couldn't be anybody but Silver.

He had had a premonition that he might want to take a holiday abroad and had got his passport fixed up when he first came out of the Army. The next thing, was to cash a cheque for five pounds. But before he went down to Folkestone that night he put through a telephone call to Mrs Byrne.

'I want you to tell me, Mrs Byrne,' he said, 'if you think I've done the wrong thing letting Silver go.'

A little laugh from Mrs Byrne from whom Sylvia had inherited much of her charm, and she had always liked Johnny.

'Of course it was wrong, and Sylvia's been very unhappy. She needs you. Besides, my husband believes in you.'

'But if I buzz down to Monte and join her, will she want to see me?'

'I should think,' came the answer, 'that she will be absolutely thrilled. You go, Johnny, with my blessing. I can tell you the route they intended to take. Kay had it all worked out.'

And Johnny went, his heart singing like a bird and his whole world changed. He left his financial worries, his problems as a doctor and his foolish pride behind him. And now to find the right route.

Sylvia and Kay had had twenty-four hours' start by the time he got to Paris, and a bit more by the time he was joined by Bob, who was in tremendous form — just feeling, he said, like a few days of sunshine and Continental cooking.

The two young men, very English-looking in their sports shirts and grey flannels, each with a pipe in his mouth, sat on the front seat of a bright green 10-h.p. van, said to have one of the fastest, most economical engines in the trade, and joined the stream of limousines, coaches, and cars of all sorts heading for the South.

'Object — ' said Johnny, 'to overtake one short, fair girl and one tall, dark one, carrying rucksacks on their backs! They may walk a bit. More likely they'll have cadged lifts. But we can make enquiries here and there at the places they'll probably have stopped at.'

'Don't worry, old son,' said Bob. 'If we don't have any luck before — we'll find them in Monte Carlo.'

6

On the previous day, Sylvia and Kay were given a lift by an elderly Frenchman, travelling in wines, who took them as far as Fontainebleau.

The delicate green of that loveliest, most romantic of French forests made Sylvia feel she wanted to stay there. It fitted in with her present mood of amorous melancholy. But Kay urged her on. They must try to cover at least three hundred kilometres a day, she said. So they walked around the town; stood awhile in the square where Napoleon once reviewed his troops in front of the great iron gates of the Château. When they bade farewell to this nostalgic splendour they were in a shabby English pre-war relic of a car driven by two elderly ladies who were wending their way to Aix-en-Provence. And this time they got almost as far as

Vezelay, but there the 'relic' broke down. The elderly spinster who was the driver railed in execrable French at a garage mechanic because he could not start the engine again. Sylvia and Kay, amused, but with no intention of being drawn into the argument, offered their thanks and walked on toward the *Basilica de la Madeleine*, an old and magnificent monastery on the hill. Kay was enjoying herself, taking an interest in everything. Sylvia less so because she couldn't get Johnny out of her mind, and also because she had a delicate skin which had caught the sun already. She began to feel hot and tired.

They returned to the main road where they found a café on the roadside and sat at a table under a big chestnut tree, drinking *café filtre*. To their left stretched a long straight road fringed by rows of tall poplars, and another few hours' journey to Dijon.

'I must put some cream on my face,' said Sylvia, and rummaged in her rucksack. Last night she had been too unhappy to take much notice of the contents. Now suddenly she saw the unfamiliar pink tube marked Cool-creem.

'Where on earth did that come from? I must be 'nuts', but I don't remember buying it.'

Kay picked it up.

'Oh, it's grand stuff. I always use it at home. Probably Aunt Lil slipped it into your rucksack. But don't open it if it's a new one. I've started on mine and they go dry. Here you are!'

Sylvia put the unopened tube in her rucksack and applied some of the cream from her cousin's tube on to hot cheeks and pink-tinged shoulders. It had been so warm that morning she had worn a sun-bathing cotton top and now regretted it. She must certainly put on the bolero for the rest of the day.

It was at this precise moment that the powerful Citröen carrying Lucille Renard passed through Vezelay. Lucille had just inserted a cigarette into a long ivory holder when she saw the two girls with their rucksacks outside the small café. Her heart jolted.

'*Arretez!*' she hissed at the chauffeur.

The Citröen drew up in a cloud of dust. Lucille stepped out before the café and Sylvia blinked through her sun-glasses.

'Gosh, Kay! That's how *we* ought to look! And *what* a motor!'

'And nobody in the back — we might get a luxury drive on to Dijon. What say you?'

Lucille by now had reached their table. Her scarlet lips parted in a brilliant smile.

'*Bonjour, mesdemoiselles*' — she bowed to each of the girls in turn. 'May I join you for a coffee?'

'*Avec plaisir,*' said Kay, with a frightful accent.

Thereupon Lucille, still smiling, seated herself gracefully, smoothed a pleat in her white linen skirt and fingered the sparkling clip on the lapel of a jacket that Sylvia reckoned must have been made by one of the most expensive couturiers in Paris.

'You are English? I speak it,' said Lucille. 'I was three years in London at a university studying languages.'

And Sylvia and Kay were not to know that the three years had in fact been spent as a dance hostess in a small night club in Soho where Henri Chasseur had first met Lucille. Henri was the brains and organizer of a gang of international jewel thieves. He had had some remarkable successes, operating from various seemingly innocent-looking antique shops in London, Paris and Brussels. His headquarters were in Paris, but the stolen gems were nearly always broken up and disposed of in the Château at Dijon. This place had been chosen because it was not noticeable in any way. Henri was known in the district as a connoisseur frequently away on business. The 'museum' was left in the care of a butler and his wife. The butler, incidentally, was one of the finest judges of uncut stones in the world. He worshipped Henri.

Everybody worshipped Henri for a time. He was unusually handsome and had delightful manners. The ice-cold cruelty and rapaciousness of the man became apparent only to those who dealt with him intimately and upset him. Nobody ever voluntarily crossed Henri's wishes a second time!

There had been many women in his life before Lucille. He picked them up when they amused him and dropped them when they ceased to be amusing. The kind of callousness he showed in all his dealings. Lucille had so far had a longer run than most because she managed not to irritate him. She made no emotional demands. Henri was a cold sensualist. Lucille was the same and he found her exceptional beauty and flawless figure as fascinating as one of his fabulous stolen jewels. Only she was not for sale! He kept her with him. She made a fitting companion for him when he needed a woman at his side. And she was useful in his 'business'.

There was only one thing Lucille

wanted that he had so far not given her
— marriage.

Lucille was quite certain that the two
girls with whom she had coffee were the
ones Rex Harris had described. It was
not difficult to ingratiate herself by
offering them a lift to Dijon. They
accepted, smiling at each other, because
it was what they had hoped for. Then it
was only a question of a few moments
before Lucille complained of the hot
sun.

'Just imagine — I have not brought
with me my sunburn cream,' she
sighed.

Sylvia immediately brought out Kay's
used tube of Cool-creem. Lucille's
heart jolted. She eyed with fascination
that innocent looking tube, squeezed a
very little on to the back of her hand
and smelt it. Then, with a well-acted
show-of enthusiasm, she begged Sylvia
to sell it to her.

'Nevair can I get this cream in
France. It is an English make and
dee-licious. If *Mademoiselle* will accept

two or three hundred francs — I would like to buy it. Oh, yes, please, *please*. You can buy many English makes, but this one for me is exceptional.'

Sylvia stared a little. How extraordinary! The elegant Parisienne to be so keen on a silly tube of sun cream. She looked at Kay who whispered:

'Okay. Let her have it! We need the francs and we've got the other tube!'

Lucille was thinking:

'The emeralds must be at the bottom. *Mon Dieu!* Already they have begun to use it — what a stroke of luck I have found them — only just in time. And it is the brand Rex mentioned. There can be no doubt.'

Without further ado the exchange was made. Two hundred francs found their way into Sylvia's purse and the tube of cream into Lucille's. After which Lucille was in glowing form. Henri was going to be very pleased with her tonight. She could not wait to get down to the Château.

The girls were only too willing to set

off again, and took their seats in the beautiful car. As they drove along they chattered gaily. Lucille was interested in the Coronation. Kay answered most of her questions. But Sylvia looked at the countryside, the rolling pastures, the little clumps of forests on little hills, the isolated farms. This was her first real glimpse of France. England had receded and with it the life she used to live at home. But at the back of her mind there was always the memory of Johnny.

They reached Dijon at twilight. Lucille, brilliant with smiles, graciously directed her chauffeur to drive the girls to a small, inexpensive hotel called *Les Trois Ours*. It was a sixteenth-century inn facing a delightful square flanked by plane trees. Gaily crowded this evening because there had been a market today and it was just breaking up. It was all so colourful, so unlike anything she had seen before, Sylvia was fascinated by it. The girls deposited their ruck-sacks in the small room overlooking the square and went out to explore.

'What a fascinating woman that was!' Kay remarked, remembering Lucille. 'Such a pity she wasn't going on to Monte. I could have done with another ride in that Citröen!'

'Oh, well — three cheers for English Cool-creem — it will pay for part of our dinner this evening,' said Sylvia.

The Cool-creem meanwhile was being rushed by Lucille in her car up a small hill on the outskirts of the town to a gloomy old house known as the *Château des Pines*. It was partly concealed by pine trees, approached through wrought-iron gates. The much-neglected gardens were surrounded by a high wall. The Château itself looked shabby and forlorn on the outside with its peeling paint and air of decay. But inside it was beautiful. *Le petit musée*. A veritable store of treasures.

Lucille, her face bursting with excitement, did not waste time greeting the butler who opened the great studded door which was heavily barred.

'*Monsieur* is in?' she demanded.

'*Oui mademoiselle*, in the library — '

Lucille half ran into the room. Her large sparkling eyes focused on Henri, whom she found seated at a big Louis XV desk. He was examining a small *objet d'art* through a magnifying glass. A huge Alsatian lay on the rug at his feet. The animal rose and growled as Lucille entered. It was Henri's pet, but did not like Lucille and she was afraid of it.

'Get rid of that brute,' she demanded.

Henri looked up.

He was an elegantly dressed man approaching forty, with smooth fair hair and eyes of such a pale blue as to be startling in contrast to his dark tan. He had an almost mesmeric gaze — deep and unwavering. It was not a good face in repose but he had a charming smile. He smiled now at Lucille, rose, opened the french windows and sent the dog out.

'Such a pity you are not a lover of animals, *ma chére.*' he murmured. 'But I am delighted to see you. You should spend more time in the country at this time of year. I must arrange for it. You have come, I presume, because you have the emeralds?'

Triumphantly she produced the tube of cream and flung it on the desk.

'You told me not to come until I *did* find them.'

Henri did not touch the tube for a moment. He busied himself lighting a cigarette. The extraordinarily blue eyes were turned upon the tube of cream, not the beautiful woman.

'How did you get it?' He snapped the words.

She told him whilst she drew off her jacket and straightened her linen skirt. She was hot and longing for a drink. But first — to business. Henri would never allow himself a drink, or an hour of dalliance with her, until he had got those small green stones which he so badly wanted.

He listened to Lucille's story, nodding now and again. Then he took a large sheet of blotting paper, spread it in front of him and began to squeeze the tube of cream, emptying it slowly, gently. Fascinated and absorbed, Lucille watched until the white spiral had been forced from the pink container. Bit by bit her feeling of elation died. The colour left her cheeks. She saw Henri take a pencil and spread out the cream. She saw the blue steady gaze that she dreaded yet which she found so irresistible turn upon her. Then in a quiet voice, Henri said:

'*Where are the emeralds?*'

She sprang up and stuttered:

'But I don't understand. That is the tube! That is the name of the cream! Rex told me! There can't be any mistake. They were the two girls — who came over on his boat — I ascertained it beyond all doubt. *Mon Dieu!*'

Now suddenly the silence of the quiet library where no sunlight ever penetrated because the pine trees grew so close to the windows — was shattered by a violent crash of Henri's fist on the desk.

'*Imbecile!* You have made a fool of yourself and me! The emeralds are not here.'

'But they must be!' Lucille choked.

'They are not. Look for yourself.'

'Then Rex has kept them and double-crossed you.'

'No. He spoke to me a few moments ago from Paris. They have released him and he is on his way here. He would not dare to double-cross me.'

'But they were the same girls — from his description I know it — the tall dark one and the short fair one. I tell you it was they,' said Lucille despairingly.

Henri's handsome face was a mask of rage. He snarled:

'Then these so-called innocent pair of girls have already squeezed out the emeralds and stuck to them. Where are these girls, now?'

'Staying at *Les Trois Ours.*'

'You will go back at once and

investigate. You will find those emeralds, *ma chére* Lucille, or . . . ' he broke off significantly.

Sylvia and Kay sat under the awning of the café of *Les Trois Ours* facing the square and watched the moon-light dip into the fountain, until the spray looked like crystallizing diamonds.

They had enjoyed their food. *Hors d'œuvres*, crisp green salad in a wooden bowl that had been rubbed with garlic; and perfect juicy steak washed down by the local burgundy.

An American — a big, blond man with the square, school-boy face and rangy figure of his race — drove up in a huge Cadillac. A powerful cream-coloured monster that soon brought an admiring crowd around it.

The American also having booked a room at *Les Trois Ours* settled himself down to a gargantuan meal. From the beginning he noticed the two girls, and decided that both of them were attractive and that what he needed was a 'sugar-baby' for the remainder of the drive to Cannes where he was meeting his family.

'Scram you kids — *allez vous en!*' he said with a good-natured grin at the little boys clambering around the Cadillac, then grinned at the girls. 'Hiya!' he added. 'Swell place this. Way back home they've heard about *Les Trois Ours*. Been here long?'

Kay, nearly always the spokesman, answered and told him they had only just arrived. Soon they were all three discussing that subject of international interest — food. The American introduced himself as Royce Hammond and insisted on them having coffee and cognac with him.

Afterwards he volunteered to take them both sight-seeing. They wandered off on foot. All of them had had enough driving for one day. The man's merry, amorous gaze wandered rather more often than not to Sylvia. Her charming face and head with the classic short-cut waves of pale gilt hair fascinated him. But he got small response from her so turned his attention to the handsome brunette. Kay was more reciprocative. When he asked in a whisper why the little 'blonde' was so melancholy, Kay laughed and whispered back:

'Oh, just a love affair that's gone wrong.'

He shook his head.

'Say! Love affairs so often go wrong at the beginning and at the end. It's the middle stretch seems best,' he observed.

Sylvia heard the two whispering and came to the conclusion she was odd man out. The ache in her heart for Johnny was growing worse. She decided to go back to the hotel alone and write to her mother.

'You two carry on looking around. I'll be okay,' she said.

7

Just before this, Lucille, unusually nervous and intimidated by Henri's furious show of anger and disappointment, drove down to *Les Trois Ours* and asked if she might see the two English ladies whom she had dropped there earlier in the day. The manager knew Lucille. He also knew Monsieur Chasseur, who had a good reputation and paid all his bills. He informed the elegant Parisienne politely that the young English ladies had just gone out for a walk with an American *monsieur*.

Lucille's brain worked swiftly. Had they taken their, rucksacks? Probably not. She suggested that she was a great friend of theirs and would like to run up to see if by any chance they had returned unnoticed to their room. The *patron* bowed his acquiescence.

Lucille darted upstairs to Room 9.

Her eyes glittered in a fever of impatience as she made a thorough search through every drawer and in the two rucksacks which were there on the floor. They had only been partially unpacked. She left nothing to chance. She went through every box, bag and pot. There were no emeralds. She even sifted through the face powder, searching wildly in case there should be another tube of Cool-creem, which was a possibility. But she found nothing. With a sinking heart — genuinely bewildered — Lucille returned the room to its former order, and then drove back to the Château. She was in for a bad time with Henri, she was sure. She dreaded what he would say — and do. And she was also quite certain that it was Rex Harris — that little *cochon* — who had double-crossed them. Whereas it so happened that the tube was merely reposing in the bag Sylvia carried when she went out with Kay.

Henri was brief and ruthless in his treatment of Lucille after she returned with her bad news.

He still believed that the Englishman, Harris, was not the thief. In his opinion those two girls were less innocent than they appeared. He surmised that they had found the gems and either taken them to the police or still had them in their possession, perhaps in one of their *sacs*.

'*Pas possible!*' muttered Lucille.

Henri lit a cigar.

'You will sit down and write a note in English and you will suggest that the young ladies might lunch with us tomorrow and look at my museum. I wish to have them here, and speak with them myself. Send Marcel to *Les Trois Ours* with the note and tell him to wait for a reply.'

Her sloe-dark eyes glowered at him.

'You want them *here*?'

'Yes, and you will prepare a delightful lunch and be a charming hostess — my sister, Mlle Chausseur.'

She walked up to him and put her arms around his neck.

'I will do as you say, *chéri*, but do not be cross with me. It is not my fault! The mistake is not mine.'

He took her wrists and pushed her away without ceremony. She lost balance a little and the Alsatian leapt out suddenly from under the desk, barking at her. Henri gave a low laugh. He looked most handsome, most gay. But Lucille sat down and trembled violently — her nerves ragged. She was afraid of the dog and terrified that Henri was no longer in love with her. He seemed only too anxious to attach the blame for the missing emeralds to *her*. She made no further attempt to conciliate him. She knew him too well. There were tears of rage in her eyes as she started with shaking hand to write the invitation to the English girls.

This letter was brought to Sylvia half an hour after she had returned to the inn. Not to bed, for she was restless and trying to fight the inclination to sit down and write to Johnny as well as to her parents. The letter from 'Mlle

Chausseur' both surprised and interested her. The lovely Parisienne had even been down in person to try to find them, so the *Patron* had just informed her. Everybody knew, he had said, that *Monsieur* Chasseur had some very beautiful treasures in the Château. They had been asked to lunch! That would be exciting — a lunch in a private château, as guests of a real connoisseur. Sylvia adored antiques. As for pushing on at breakneck speed to cover all these kilometres a day — why worry? What was the rush?

Without waiting for Kay, Sylvia wrote out an acceptance and sent it down to the waiting butler.

Henri could be irresistible to women when he chose. When the two English girls arrived for lunch, he concentrated on being the perfect host.

Kay, too, had thought this a fine idea. First of all the weather had changed overnight — Dijon lay steaming under a mist of summer rain which did not induce them to hurry on their way.

Secondly, Royce Hammond had offered to take them later this afternoon in the marvellous Cadillac as far as Cannes. Which mean that there would be no more having to trudge on foot or thumb a lift. Kay and Royce had got on very well. The Australian girl was in fine spirits. It was arranged that they should all set out from Dijon about three o'clock. They should make Lyons by nightfall.

The girls had decided to go to the lunch party at the *Château des Pines* a little more 'dressed' than usual. Sylvia looked her most attractive in a daffodil-yellow floral dress that had a wide, short skirt bunching out from her small waist. She was very much in the foreground today because she knew quite a lot about the treasures Monsieur Chasseur displayed to her. He was delighted by her knowledge. He also allowed his mind to deviate for a moment from the thought of the two million francs worth of missing emeralds and centre upon the enchanting

Sylvia. She was so little and feminine — so refreshing after the blasé, sophisticated Lucille. A rare treasure in these days — he would like to add her to his collection.

Lucille, too, played the perfect hostess, but her spirits went down to zero. Fiendish jealousy possessed her as she listened and watched. She knew Henri so well — that tender, gentle way in which he hung over Sylvia as he explained pictures and books and let her hold some of his fabulous china. His genuine admiration when the young girl, as soon as she arrived, had walked up to Setti, the Alsatian, knelt down and put her arms around the dog's sleek neck.

'Oh, you *adorable* thing!' she exclaimed.

Setti wagged his tail and laid his pointed muzzle on her shoulder. Henri's pale blue eyes sparkled wickedly at Lucille who returned the gaze with malevolence. And that was the moment in which Henri Chausseur decided that he wanted Sylvia whether she had the emeralds or not.

During the exquisite lunch which was served in the big, handsome dining-room, he questioned both the girls about their channel crossing, and in such a delicate way that he managed to extract from Kay all the information he needed about Rex Harris. It confirmed Rex's story of the meeting with the girls.

'That horrid little man who tried to get into our taxi!' was Sylvia's contribution to the tale.

Henri concealed a smile at the thought of the 'horrid little man'. Rex Harris had done one or two excellent jobs for him. This was the first time he had slipped up — *if it were he who had slipped!*

But *if* those emeralds had ever been in the girls' possession and — they had discovered them — and *if* they were the innocuous tourists they appeared to be — surely they would have mentioned the discovery to him, Henri, as part of their adventure.

But not a word was said — not a clue could Henri discover. He even asked Sylvia blandly if *Mademoiselle* Sylvia liked emeralds and watched her face while she answered:

'What woman doesn't? But I've never had any — they're too expensive. But I love Mummy's engagement ring. That's an emerald.' She spoke with a naïve frankness that impressed him.

Lucille pulled him aside.

'You're wasting your time. They know nothing!'

Henri looked speculatively at Sylvia's pale gilt head and the sprinkle of golden freckles on her *retroussé* nose.

'*Comme elle est ravissante!* Like an untouched flower,' he murmured.

Lucille clenched her teeth. If Henri started to be romantic it was certainly the beginning of the end. Time was flying by and the English girls had a date with the American who was giving them a lift. They went into Lucille's ornate and gold bedroom to powder before departing.

'We won't change again — we can sit in the Cadillac as we are,' said Kay.

'What a delightful man M. Chausseur is,' Sylvia remarked.

'I think he's rather odd; in fact this whole château is a bit queer,' said Kay.

'Oh, why? I've enjoyed it *immensely*,' said Sylvia 'I'm feeling much better this morning!'

Which showed, Kay remarked dryly, what a good-looking, attractive Frenchman could do in a couple of hours!

Sylvia opened her bag and took out the new tube of Cool-creem.

'Henri is sweet. I say, Kay, I'm not going to risk another burning. The sun's coming out again and it'll be terrifically hot with this humidity.'

She found the cream difficult to extract. Something was sticking. She squeezed hard and the tube burst. There emerged a spiral of cream. She applied it to her face and throat before she came to what looked like a piece of coloured glass sticky with cream. She

106

took no interest in it but stuck it on to a tissue and left it on the dressing-table, then wrapped the tube in a clean tissue and returned it to her bag.

'These tubes do break easily these days,' she remarked to Kay, 'and the beastly stuff has bits of glass in it. I've a jolly good mind to send the tube back to the manufacturer. It's frightfully expensive stuff and I don't see why one should have to put up with this sort of thing. Imagine if you rubbed broken glass into your face what might happen.'

'I agree honey,' said Kay; 'let's pack it up and send it right now.'

'Well, I'll wait and see if there's any more glass,' said Sylvia. 'You can't buy this stuff in France and everyone says it is the best, and you know how easily I burn.'

Downstairs Henri kissed her hand in farewell and escorted the girls to his car, which was taking them back to *Les Trois Ours*.

'I think,' he murmured, 'I must come

down to Monte. I would like so *very* much to see you again. You like dancing, perhaps? Would you dine and dance with me one evening at the Sporting Club if I take a little holiday?'

Now Sylvia was not being disloyal to her memory of Johnny when she responded to this invitation. But really, M. Chausseur overwhelmed her with his charm and his fascinating culture! And it *was* nice to know that *some* man was sufficiently interested to want to follow you a few hundred miles.

She answered Henri in the affirmative.

After they had driven away, Lucille let forth a stream of protest.

'What have you found out? Nothing! They had not got the emeralds. That is obvious. And you — making an imbecile of yourself over that insipid English brat! *Bon Dieu!*'

He turned to her, his eyes narrowed to pinpoints.

'I have had enough of you, Lucille, *ma très chère*', he said in a frozen voice.

'It is you who are a brat. You must remember that I picked you up in the lowest of dance-halls and made you what you are today. But you can return to your former insignificance. Lately you have been worse than useless and a bore. I shall speak to Rex when he arrives but I still think it is you who have bungled this affair. As for the little Sylvia — Setti likes her. That is v-e-ree important! What a heavenly sight — when she embraced him without fear! As I would like to embrace her — my arms around her — so . . . '

He spoke dreamily, gesticulating. Then his tone changed. He snarled at Lucille:

'Those emeralds have got to be found or you and Harris will both pay for it.'

For an hour they wrangled bitterly. At the end, Henri, in one of his most villainous moods, slapped her across the face and ordered her to her room. Lucille burst into a storm of tears and rushed to her room. She flung herself on to the stool before her dressing-table. Her mascara was running. Her beauty was disfigured. She had never loved Henri. She had known only passionate desire for him and greed for the luxury in which he kept her. But to blame her like this for the loss of the emeralds and humiliate her by showing such open desire to make a new conquest filled her with murderous rage.

She picked up the cream-splashed face tissue that Sylvia had been using and was about to fling it angrily into a waste-paper basket when she saw, suddenly, the green glitter of the stone.

Lucille stopped crying. Her heart plunged. She seized the stone and wiped it clean on a face tissue. The 'foreign body' that Sylvia had not even bothered to examine was a small — very small — but flawless emerald. *An emerald.* Lucille's brow was wet. Then Rex had been right. There were plenty of bigger ones in that collection. This possibly was one of the smallest.

But it was an *emerald*. And this was the table at which Sylvia and Kay had powdered their noses. Obviously one of them had used some cream. *There had been a second tube of Cool-creem after all!*

Down flew Lucille and burst into Henri's library He was not there. He had taken Setti out. The sun, which had shone for half an hour, had receded again behind heavy clouds. A distant growl of thunder suggested the approach of a storm. Henri would be back any moment.

When Henri Chausseur strolled back with his Alsatian, the rain had begun to fall in big heavy drops. Lightning played fitfully over the old house and the wooded grounds.

Henri took one look at the stone on Lucille's out-stretched palm, transferred it carefully and without a change of expression to his note-case, then for the second time that day struck the woman across the cheek.

'*So!*' he said sibilantly. 'They have the

tube. Of course they do not know what it is, this little stone. Nor that there are others. But you have bungled the job. *You* — not Rex.'

She put a hand to her stinging face, her magnificent eyes flashing with resentment.

'It is not my fault — I tell you I did all I could to find it. The girls must have had the tube *with* them. I have been unlucky.'

'They still have it. And you will remain unlucky. You can pack your things and get out of here and out of the flat in Paris, too,' he said. 'We are finished — you and I.'

'You are going after that girl?'

'The charming little Sylvia? And two million francs' worth of emeralds — yes. *Allez!'*

He shot the last word at her contemptuously.

'They are in the American's Cadillac. It is very fast and you will never overtake them!' screamed Lucille.

'Then I shall find them in Monte

Carlo,' he said, and flung out of the room. A moment later Lucille heard the Citröen roaring down the drive through the rain.

It was about an hour later during this storm — one of the fiercest they had known in Dijon — that a small green new-looking commercial van pulled up before *Les Trois Ours*. Out of it stepped two damp, tired-looking young men — Johnny, and Bob Blunt.

'We need a drink and a night's sleep,' Bob had just said. 'This place is no luxury hotel but the food — oh, boy! I've been here before. We'll get ourselves fixed up for the night.'

Johnny eyed the stormy sky gloomily and dived through a curtain of rain into the shelter of the inn.

'You don't suppose there's the ghost of a chance Silver and her cousin stopped here, do you?' he asked.

'You never know your luck,' Bob returned cheerfully. 'Most people passing through Dijon eat here. You can but ask.'

8

And Johnny asked . . . with results that sent his hopes soaring upwards.

Two English ladies had stayed here last night. They had signed the book. Johnny inspected it. He rushed back to Bob, who was propping his large body against the small bar, drinking an English-looking mug of beer and ordering an exceedingly French dinner.

'Frog's legs, what about it, old boy?' Bob began.

Johnny broke in — eyes blue and bright:

'Silver was here last night. We're right on the track.'

Bob smacked his lips. Outside the quiet inn the thunder continued to growl. The rain spattered against the windows. His thoughts were on food and drink rather than love. But he clapped his friend on the back.

'Just the job. But don't ask me to start out again until I've had a spot of shut-eye and a good feed.'

Johnny's face fell.

'They've left with a Yank in a Cadillac. It'll be a bit of a thing overtaking *that* in our 'bus.'

Bob's roar of laughter made the *Patron* raise his brows. His wife fingered the locket that rested on her large bosom and blinked her mournful Pekinese-eyes at Bob.

'*Ces Anglaises!*' she muttered.

But her daughter, Marie, whose nightly prayer was that she might grow more and more like Michéle Morgan, slanted an admiring gaze at the two tall, handsome English boys.

Bob addressed her in poisonous French. She informed him sibilantly that Mademoiselle Lucille had brought the two English *Meeses* here, and that the English ladies had had the honour of lunching at the *Château des Pines* with Monsieur Chausseur, who was an art expert and *connoisseur des*

115

meubles. Translating this to himself, Johnny decided to call on M. Chausseur and the beautiful Mademoiselle Lucille after dinner. They would undoubtedly be able to give him up-to-date news of Silver. His longing to see Sylvia and bridge their differences had intensified with every kilometre covered by the little van.

Bob left him to it. He preferred to stay in *Les Trois Ours* and flirt with Marie.

The storm had died down. Johnny walked through the iron gateway leading into the Château just as the sun was breaking through the clouds. The earth steamed and it grew warm again. He glanced without interest at a black Renault drawn up at the side of the road. It was half concealed by poplars. But a man with a slouch hat pulled low over his brow watched the good-looking, curly-haired young man in the British sports attire stroll up the drive, and was considerably interested.

Johnny approached the old Château

and indulged in the pleasing reflection that Silver had walked along this very avenue only a few hours before him. Would she be pleased to see him when finally they met — or would she refuse to forgive his stubborn rejection of her love and tell him she had finished with him?

He rang the bell. From the back came a dog's deep-throated bark. The studded door opened cautiously.

A few moments later Johnny was seated in the library, astonished to find himself being entertained — and very charmingly — by one of the most fascinating women he had ever met.

Marcel, the butler, had just been telling Johnny that *Monsieur* was away, when Lucille passed through the hall and overheard. Immediately she invited Johnny indoors. Now they sat drinking Dubonnet together — appraising one another. Johnny preferred blondes but had to admit that Mlle Chausseur had 'everything'; that dark languorous beauty, those long slim legs, the ravishing smile. She in turn set herself out to attract Johnny. She had a heavy score up against Henri, and she had disliked Sylvia from the moment Henri had turned his attention upon her. She knew all about the Johnny — Sylvia quarrel now. She found it a matter for laughter rather than tears. The poor fools! Lucille had no time for quixotry. Nor for sacrifice. But if the English boy was guilty of the first, he was the most physically attractive of any of the young men whom Lucille had encountered for a long time.

In her queer, unpredictable feminine fashion she fell madly in love with him. She also decided to use him. Henri had left her here to find her own way back to Paris. He had dropped her like a used glove. Well, she knew now from Johnny that his travelling companion was a wealthy English manufacturer of commercial cars. Why shouldn't they take her down to Monte Carlo with them? She had a diamond bracelet she could sell there and pay her hotel bill if it wasn't paid for her. She would be sure to meet up with Henri, once she reached Monaco. His mother, blind and old and the only human being for whom he really cared, occupied a small house on the hill overlooking the sea. Henri had a good friend with a business near the Casino. He was a dealer in antiques and jewellery — yet another who received stolen goods.

It would be fun, Lucille decided, to get down there and flaunt a close friendship with these English boys. She would stay in the same hotel with them, and if she worked hard maybe she could induce Johnny to stop worrying about the stupid little English girl. He might even consent to take *her* back to London.

So ran Lucille's extravagant thoughts. And when she told Johnny that she wanted a lift to Monte Carlo, he was only too pleased to say 'yes'. He knew Bob would not mind. But he warned Lucille that it wouldn't be comfortable in a Blunt's van — if she was used to luxury travel! But at this Lucille's eyes shone and she laughed gaily.

'Ah, but we will all have su-u-ch fun!' she said and looked at him invitingly through her long, sticky lashes.

Johnny felt embarrassed but not displeased. He was less pleased, however, when Lucille asked if she might confide in him, but added that she was afraid it might upset him if he was really the fiancé of Mlle Sylvia.

'What do you mean?' he asked uneasily. 'I am not her *accepted* fiancé because I put a spanner in the works by telling her I wouldn't marry while I was still doing a hospital job and so short of cash. But' — he looked at Lucille with some perplexity — 'what goes on? I mean about *Sylvia*.'

Lucille told him then a slick little story (punctuated with apologies in case she might hurt his feelings by implying that the 'leetle' Sylvia was just a 'leetle' bit of a coquette) about her brother Henri and his infatuation for Sylvia. He was easily inflamed, she sighed. He had fallen oh! so crazily in love with Sylvia. He could be *brutal* — and to her, his sister, he had behaved *brutally*. He had even stolen her Citröen in order to follow the two girls who were with the American. With her own ears she had heard Henri and Sylvia making a date to meet in Monte Carlo. Oh, yes, obviously it was *'l'amour'* at first sight with those two.

Johnny's heart sank; his healthy face whitened and his jaw took on a rigid line.

Sylvia and a *Frenchman!* Every word that Lucille said hammered on his most sensitive feelings. How could Sylvia so soon have recovered from their misunderstanding that she found it easy to replace him? That had been the bogy that had travelled with Johnny all through his journey to the south.

He look agonized.

'I can only blame myself,' he muttered.

But Lucille said softly:

'Pardon — she cannot have been

over-serious if she can so soon find another love. But, *courage mon ami!* The world is wide and there are other loves — '

Johnny felt confused and more than unhappy. At the same time he tried to concentrate on Lucille's exquisite ankles. But he was only further depressed when she added her brother had always said he wished to marry an Englishwoman. Johnny's hopes receded a little farther into the background. But having come this far — he intended to go on. He must find Sylvia and investigate the position for himself.

Meanwhile, there was the lovely, gay Lucille who wanted to go to Monte Carlo.

He phoned Bob. Bob's answer was typical:

'It'll be a tight squeeze in the front of the van but it sounds the kind of squeeze the firm won't object to! Bring her along — I'm feeling more myself now, and if you want to carry on we'll do another 100 kms. after dinner. The

Patron tells me the Cadillac was setting out to make Lyons for the night.'

Johnny returned to Lucille, who was enchanted to hear that she was to be allowed to drive down South with the Englishmen. Perhaps Henri had found those emeralds — perhaps not, she reflected. Perhaps he really *was* interested in Sylvia. She no longer cared. She was going to get Johnny Garland and his friend right on to her side and put herself under their protection. She could imagine Henri's amazement and anger when she turned up in Monte full of smiles, instead of crawling back to Paris to look for work, which was the fate to which *he* had consigned her.

It was all arranged that she should pack, then join the boys at *Les Trois Ours*. Afterwards they would wend their way to Lyons.

Johnny was sunk in gloom as he walked down the drive and turned out of the big gateway.

He stood a moment hesitating, uncertain of his way back into town. He had come to the *Château des Pines* to find news of Silver and he had heard more than he really wanted to know, he thought miserably.

He started as a man suddenly appeared from behind a clump of bushes and confronted him. He had been lost in unhappy reflections.

'What the devil — ' he began.

'*Pardon, Monsieur*,' broke in the man, 'but I would be grateful if you would come into the Renault for a moment and allow my colleague and myself to ask you a few question.'

The man spoke respectfully and in decent English, but Johnny snapped:

'I'm an English tourist. My name's Garland. What do you want with me?'

The man turned over the lapel of his jacket and exhibited a small badge.

'Pierre Gautin of the Paris *Sûreté* at your service, *Monsieur*,' he said.

Meanwhile, Sylvia sat in the back of the Cadillac during the two hundred and forty miles which they covered at the rate of sixty miles an hour between

Dijon and Orange. She did not enjoy it. She was allergic to being driven at such high speed even in the gorgeous Cadillac. But Kay liked it and reclined at Royce Hammond's side chattering gaily the whole time. This was undoubtedly the way to get to the South, she said, and it wouldn't have been any fun hitch-hiking, for the rain fell steadily as far as Valence, blotting out the lovely countryside and the small towns through which they passed.

It was just after they had skidded round a curve leaving Montelimar, Sylvia felt her nerves snapping.

She leant forward and spoke to the American.

'Can't we slow down a bit?'

He turned his head and grinned at her.

'Nervous, honey?'

'I think the road is a bit greasy here,' she returned, and looked anxiously ahead. They were coming towards an old ruined castle which dominated a tree-clad hill. It looked romantic and beautiful. But just as they crossed a humped-back bridge over a charming little river, the back wheel skidded again and she wished she could get out. The rain had stopped and the sun was coming out again in a last feeble effort to shine before twilight. She heard Royce laughing at Kay.

'Best cure for nerves is to tread on the accelerator. Anyhow, why worry — I've never hit anything yet!'

'Famous last words — ' began Kay.

Then Sylvia went rigid and every muscle tautened. Screaming she put her hands to her face. For it was at that very instant that the big Cadillac skidded for the third time; this time it turned in a circle and crashed off the road down a little slope and into a tree.

The last thing that Sylvia heard before she lost consciousness was her cousin shouting: 'Sylvia!' A long-drawn cry of fear and anxiety.

At a quarter to seven the fickle sunlight had faded and a bluish mist hung like chiffon over the soaked pasture-lands and the long, tree-fringed road that led to Lyons.

Henri Chausseur, in the Citröen, came upon the scene of disaster just as the ambulance was driving away, taking the occupants of the wrecked car to the nearest hospital. Henri got out of the Citröen. His heart was jolting nervously. From the description he had been given it was easy to recognize the cream and red Cadillac which lay on its side near the tree looking like a melancholy pale monster that has been knocked down and out.

There were two tearing anxieties in Henri's mind . . . first the emeralds . . . then Sylvia. But the two merged into one, for the emeralds were undoubtedly on Sylvia, or if not with her, with her cousin.

Two policemen with motor cycles and a couple of men from a nearby farm were huddled together, talking. One of the policemen supplied the information Henri wanted. The American they said

had been badly hurt, but by a miracle
neither of the English ladies had sus-
tained more than a few bruises and
shock. But they had gone in the ambulance to the hospital with *Monsieur*.

'And their rucksacks have gone with
them,' reflected Henri. He drove on in
the Citröen — a little more carefully
than usual, perhaps having seen the
result of undue haste — to the address
the police had given him. The *Hôpital
du Sacré Coeur* in Orange.

He found the girls there being
given hot coffee and brandy in the
office of the matron. She was a
white-garbed nun and the hospital
apparently was run by the nuns from
the nearby Convent of the Sacred
Heart. The girls seemed delighted to
see Henri.

Kay had one arm in a sling, but the
big Australian girl was a creature of
strong nerves and, shaken though she
had been by the accident, she was
almost her normal cheerful self. Her
main anxiety had been for their

American friend, but the latest news from the doctor was that he had only slight concussion and several broken ribs. They had all three had a merciful escape. Sylvia, especially, who could complain of nothing more than having a few bruises on her back. The car door on her side had burst open and she had been flung out on to the edge of a field of wheat.

She was never to forget the accident; she suffered nightmares for some time afterwards, and it was she who had sat in the field with Royce's head on her lap while Kay walked to the farmhouse for help.

The girls were surprised as well as relieved to see their friend from the *Château des Pines*. He wrung each of their hands in turn and expressed his horror and concern, letting his blue mesmeric gaze rest longest upon Sylvia. He pressed one of her small hands warmly between his.

'*Mon Dieu!* Imagine what I felt when I came upon the wreck!' he exclaimed, then added in a low voice, 'You see, I had to follow you at once. I could not wait to see you again.'

Sylvia gave a feeble smile. She was feeling weak and stupid after the shock of the accident. She found it rather pleasant to stop worrying about Johnny — or anything else — and M. Chausseur was so soothing. Later they were told they could do nothing for Royce Hammond. He had not recovered consciousness, but the police were communicating with his family in Cannes. There was no object in the girls' remaining here and Sylvia was anxious to get away from the hospital. Kay equally so. When Henri suggested he should find them rooms for the night at a good hotel which he knew in Orange, they agreed and allowed him to think and plan for them.

Tomorrow, he said, he would drive them oh! so slowly and carefully on to Avignon and the South.

'Poor Royce Hammond,' sighed Kay,

as they drove down the hill from the hospital, 'what a dreadful thing to have happened.'

'But thanks be to God that you have escaped,' said Henri.

He was charming, friendly, helpful, and arranged everything in the Hotel Royale, which they found small but comfortable.

But now Henri's thoughts were not so much with Sylvia's beauty and feminine appeal as with the emeralds.

Where was that tube of sunburn cream? Henri's fingers itched to unstrap both the rucksacks that he had lifted out of his car and handed to the girls. But to make it so obvious that he wanted that cream was something he dared not do. It would seem too ridiculous and be too dangerous. He could not share with them the secret of those little green stones in the tube. If they knew they would talk. And he could not risk drawing the attention of the police to himself. There was too much activity going on; a leak in the security measures taken by his own gang.

He had had a telephone call from Flick, his London representative. Flick had organized, very carefully, the theft of the emeralds in the first place. One of the boys had 'coshed' the jeweller who left Hatton Garden with the stones in his possession. The trouble had all started when Flick's girl-friend, known as 'Platinum Pam', had quarrelled with him and informed Scotland Yard. So much Henri knew — little else; except that Rex had been traced and held for questioning. He, having planted the emeralds on the English girls and been found with nothing on him, had got away. It was possible they might all get through if they were lucky. But they would have to be careful. And if the finger of suspicion eventually pointed at Henri, it would be a useful 'blind' if he could attach himself to the English girls as their travelling companion and remain attached to them. He might even return to England with them. He had a score to settle with Flick for allowing that damned platinum 'moll' of his to squeal. Henri reflected bitterly that all women were treacherous.

One thing he had decided upon; while the hue and cry was on, it would not be safe to try and dispose of the emeralds even through his trusted friend in Monte Carlo.

Better, therefore, satisfy himself that the tube of cream was still in the haversack of one of these presumably unsuspecting young ladies — *and let it stay there*. Sooner or later when he considered it the right moment, he could appropriate it.

The next difficulty was how to enquire about the sunburn cream without arousing Sylvia's or Kay's suspicions. Already Lucille had coaxed them to sell her the first tube. They would begin to think it very queer that there should be such intense interest shown in the second.

Meanwhile Johnny and Bob, with their exceedingly elegant passenger seated jubilantly between them, sped down the same wet, greasy road that had been taken by the ill-fated Cadillac.

No such tragedy occurred to Blunt's van. Although Bob's method of driving was much the same as Royce Hammond's, he had only a 10-h.p. van to drive. As he remarked to Johnny, he was 'flogging the engine disgracefully,' wilfully forgetting that it was new. By the time they got to Monte he would probably have wrecked it. But the irrepressible Bob was willing to answer to Papa for that crime.

It was Bob who did most of the talking. Johnny remained unusually quiet. But every now and then he looked sideways at Lucille's beautiful chiselled profile and shook his head as though baffled. When Lucille moved she shed about her an intoxicating odour of 'Diorama' and once when she whispered: 'Are you glad I am with you, Johnee?' he automatically responded: 'Of course!'; but shied a little from the touch of the cool, slender hand which she laid lightly on his knee.

'Why are you so quiet, *mon petit docteur?*' she demanded. 'Can you not stop thinking of your Sylvia? I assure you that she and my brother — '

But he cut this short. He had heard enough about Sylvia and Lucille's brother. He excused himself for his silence on the grounds that he had a *migraine*. But what he actually suffered from was a mind teeming with the things which had been said outside the Château, between himself and M. Gautin of the *Sûreté*.

It was a conversation which had interested him vastly and would in ordinary circumstances have appealed to his love of adventure. It was as though he had been asked to take part in a 'thriller', and it was one he would have been amused to play but for the disquieting belief that he had lost Sylvia. There were several things he wanted to ask old Bob, but he couldn't because Gautin had cautioned him to absolute silence and secrecy. So he had to keep his thoughts very much to himself. And his change of feelings toward Lucille, too. She no longer appeared quite so glamorous now that he knew that she was not Henri Chausseur's innocent sister but his far from innocent and discarded mistress.

9

It so happened that Blunt's van came upon the wrecked Cadillac early the next morning. The two young men and their French companion had spent the night at Lyons. When dawn broke the weather had changed again and it was as golden and sparkling as champagne. The van covered the 200 kms. to Orange and after crossing the hump-backed bridge came upon the mournful sight of the abandoned Cadillac, which had not yet been towed into town. A sharp cry from Johnny, and Bob pulled up the van. Johnny had been the first to see the derelict car. His healthy face changed colour.

'Oh, *God!* he said under his breath.

Lucille stared at the wreck and religiously crossed herself. Bob stopped smiling and said:

'Keep your hair on, Johnny. What

you're thinking may not be right!'

'But it *may!*' said Johnny. 'And I've got to find out.'

It wasn't difficult to discover the old farmhouse a quarter of a mile away. There, with Lucille as interpreter, they learned what had actually taken place last night. The van went on — up the hill and the *Hôpital du Sacré Coeur*. There they found that Royce Hammond was still unconscious. But the matron gave them the reassuring news of Sylvia and Kay, the only news that Johnny really wanted. Although the driver had been hurt, Silver had been thrown clear, and Cousin Kay had little more than a strained tendon and bruised elbow. What was more, he further discovered that the girls had been taken to the *Hôtel Royale* for the night.

'Now you can start grinning again, fella!' said Bob.

But when Johnny heard the name of the Frenchman who had escorted the girls to the *Hôtel Royale*, his grin rapidly faded. It was Lucille's turn to twist her voluptuous lips into a cynical smile.

'*Voila!* The leetle Sylvia is in the care of my dear brother, Henri. What did I tell you, Johnee? He was crazy for her and she for him. They are together.'

Johnny made no reply. He thrust out his jaw and narrowed his gaze. Once more in the van, on their way, Lucille snuggled up against him and sighed. He was deliciously strong; like a big, big handsome schoolboy, and she longed to make him take her in his arms. She was playing her new act so well that she was becoming quite sincere about it. She had decided to mend her ways. There would be no more emeralds and diamond bracelets and acting as hostess to criminals. Henri had finished with her, well *she* had finished with *him*. Now it might be *verree* nice to marry a sweet Englishman. Doctors were especially fascinating! She thrust a blue-veined wrist out to him.

'Johnee, feel Lucille's pulse. How

rapid it is,' she whispered.

He took the wrist and felt the beat of her pulse — with a sidelong glance that might have been described as derisive. But Lucille did not mind. She was enjoying herself and this amusing jaunt in the commercial van hugely.

They did not find the Citröen at the *Royale*. They were too late by a couple of hours. The stout *Patron* of the *Royale* informed them that the English young ladies had driven away with *Monsieur* quite early because they wished to reach Aix-en-Provence and travel slowly — the better to enjoy the beauty of Provence on this fresh June morning.

Here Lucille made a suggestion.

'I know Henri. He will take them to the *Roi René* — the best hotel in Aix. We will find them there.'

'Press on regardless,' said Bob cheerfully.

But they had a bit of bad luck. The new vehicle let them down soon after they left Avignon. The pace Bob had been setting was too much for the little van. It came to a full stop with a horrible odour of binding brakes. Bob dared not go on, but gloomily thumbed a lift back to Avignon and returned with a breakdown gang. The mechanics at the biggest and best garage were sympathetic but told Bob that it meant a removal of all brake-drums and a cleaning out of the braking system. While Bob was discussing it, Lucille and Johnny, who had also returned to Avignon by now, sat in a café in the bright sunshine and drank black coffee. Lucille displayed her fabulous legs, she was enjoying herself. But Johnny fretted and fumed. His one desire was to proceed — and find Sylvia and the others.

But it was a good few hours before they were able to drive on in the van and head South again. They had lost five hours. Darkness was veiling the lovely colourful Cézanne country-side before they entered Aix-en-Provence.

Lucille smiled at Johnny through her lashes and said in an ecstatic voice:

'It ees an *adorable* place this, and we can all go to the Casino tonight, Johnee, where we can dance!'

'Listen, folks,' said Bob good-humouredly, 'I'm only the odd man out in this set up. Let's hope that cousin of Sylvia's notices that I'm breathing! Then we might *all* dance at the Casino!'

'Henri *adores* dancing, too,' added Lucille with a wicked and significant glance at Johnny's stubborn jawline. 'Does Sylvia?'

But he pretended not to have heard the question.

As soon as she reached the *Hôtel Roi René*, Kay went to bed. Her arm was aching and she had a slight temperature which dimmed the big brunette's natural buoyancy a little. But she was quite cheerful about it, and while Sylvia helped her undress assured her there was nothing to worry about.

'I'll be right as rain in the morning. I

never go sick for long. As for you, I'm sure M. Chausseur will look after you this evening!'

Sylvia nodded. She walked over to one of the tall windows and looked down at a garden full of flowers. So far she had barely had a chance to enjoy the delights of the Provençal landscape. Henri had kept his word and driven remarkably sedately, but her nerves were still jumping. She had received only a vague impression of long stretches of golden corn rippling in the summer breeze, of fields of the burning scarlet poppies so beloved by the painter, Van Gogh. Of vineyards down in the valley; the silver green of the olive trees. Once in the charming little town itself, Henri drove them down a wide avenue flanked by plane trees and showed them the fountain in the Square. It was floodlit at night, he had told them.

'Perhaps, if you feel better, you will let me give you both dinner here, and we can listen to the music — or dance

— or gamble — whatever you will!' he had said.

He seemed quite an old friend now. And Sylvia could not pretend that the charming, cultured Frenchman did not desire something more than friendship. He seemed never to wish to leave her side. She supposed if she had any sense she would put the memory of Dr J. V. Garland right out of her mind and take what fun life offered.

'Honestly, Kay!' she exclaimed, turning round to her cousin who was now in bed and finding it blissfully comfortable relaxing between the cool coarse, linen sheets, 'we seem to have had one adventure on top of another ever since we left home. I feel quite *dazed*.'

'It certainly hasn't been quite the peaceful hitch-hike we imagined,' said Kay drowsily, 'but at least we haven't been bored! That skid in the Cadillac is the only episode I would willingly have done without. Poor Royce! I do hope he'll be all right. We must ring up the Convent tomorrow and find out.'

Sylvia sat down in front of the dressing-table. She looked at her face. It was burnt to a shade of rich golden tan. It made her hair look more bleached than ever. She shook her head at this reflection.

'My cheeks do burn!' she murmured.

'Where's the Cool-creem?' from Kay.

'In my bag. But now the tube's burst, and after finding that bit of glass, I'm a bit fed up with Cool-creem. I rolled the tube up in a tissue. Tonight I think I'll chuck it away. I'll try a bottle of suntan oil instead.'

No answer from Kay. She was drifting into a feverish slumber. After a moment Sylvia slipped off her dress, stretched herself out on the other bed, and she, too, fell asleep.

She woke to hear *la femme de chambre* tapping on the door.

'*Monsieur* asks if *Mademoiselle* is coming down,' the girl called out.

Sylvia glanced at the figure in the twin bed beside her. Kay was still sleeping soundly. Sylvia decided to let her stay that way. It was six o'clock. The sun was no longer pouring into the room and it was much cooler.

'Tell *Monsieur* I will be down in about half an hour,' said Sylvia.

When she got up she felt a good deal better. Her nerves had calmed down. The depression over Johnny, which had so far spoiled the fun of the whole journey, coupled with the horror of yesterday's accident, had done little to help revive the old Sylvia who used to be so gay and enthusiastic. As she hastily changed into the one and only cocktail dress she had brought — dark blue lace with a velvet bow at the throat, she reflected:

'Life's odd! One can soon recover one's nerve after a car smash. But when you lose the man you love — *if* you really love him — nothing, *nothing* makes you feel any better.'

She tied a blue velvet ribbon in the silver of her hair, rouged her lips and told herself that she was just a little fool. Why not make up her mind to enjoy this evening, which was to be a tête-à-tête with M. Chausseur? After all, he had taken a great deal of trouble to be nice to them; and it was a privilege seeing France through the eyes of a Frenchman who was such a delightful escort.

Sylvia sprayed a little perfume on her throat and went downstairs, bent on making the best of things.

Henri took her out on to the terrace for an aperitif. His strange eyes had kindled at the sight of the girl in her charming blue dress. He, too, wished to make the most of this evening. It was a pleasant novelty to play the part of *chevalier* to a young English girl. All that was vicious and evil in the man was temporarily subdued. Let this be a Provençal idyll in the true romantic vein, he decided. Perhaps when he had got over this tricky patch he might even consider 'selling out' — and retire gracefully from the dangerous career of the master criminal. He had some money put away, as well as the Paris flat, the Château in Dijon, and a small yacht lying off Monte Carlo. Why not settle down with an enchanting English wife? No more Lucilles in his life, no more big 'hauls' (which would mean no more risks). Just Sylvia and Setti — and the well-ordered existence of a respectable and happily married man.

While they sipped their aperitifs and talked together, Henri became so infatuated with his new design for living that he almost forgot the emeralds.

He would have given a great deal to know where that important and elusive tube of cream was at this very moment, but without giving himself away he dared not ask.

During dinner he heard all about Johnny.

They lingered over an exquisite meal on the terrace of the restaurant adjoining the Casino. A full moon silvered the trees. Music played softly in the background. Henri raised his glass of champagne to Sylvia, looking at her with much the same respect and pleasure that he would award to one of his art treasures. He assured her that she was wasting her time fretting over a *gauche* young doctor who couldn't afford to marry her.

'*Oublier!* Try to forget,' he murmured.

'I don't find it easy,' said Sylvia, sighing.

'I would like to help you,' he said, and put out a hand and covered one of hers.

She drew it back but her eyes remained soft, and she really did feel that M. Chausseur was a most attractive man and that it was very romantic out here under the stars.

She continued to think so when he took her into the Casino to dance. His dancing was superb and it was a pastime Sylvia enjoyed above all others. And they were still dancing when three people, two young men and a fashionable Parisienne, stepped out of a green and white van — a comic sight for the citizens of Aix-en-Provence — and walked into the Casino.

The trio had already been to the *Roi René*. They knew now that they had caught up with the others. Johnny had a slightly nervous air as he looked round the room. *Suddenly he saw her.* Silver, at last; scarcely the forlorn Silver he might have expected breaking her heart for *him*. This was a radiant Silver, dancing like a girl in a dream, held tightly in the arm of an exceedingly good-looking, debonair man. Johnny knew, before Lucille told him, that it was Henri Chausseur. Then Lucille gripped his arm and gave a wicked little laugh.

'So! My brother and leetle Sylvia — they get on fine — *hein*?'

Johnny clenched his hands.

It was Bob Blunt's turn to size up the situation. He did a lot of laughing but he took in most things that were happening. He knew quite well how Johnny Garland felt at this moment. In a low voice, Bob said:

'Take it easy, fella. Why don't you

and Lucille go dancing? I think I'll have a small gamble in the *Salla de Jeu*. See you later.'

Johnny stood rigid. His feelings were mixed. But his relief that Sylvia looked so well and had obviously suffered no ill effects from the accident were blurred by intense jealousy and dislike of the Frenchman.

Lucille pouted.

'I warned you, Johnee. But do not let her think you mind. Come, *chéri*, dance with me!'

He had a moment's struggle with himself. He tried to concentrate on the memory of a number of cautions given him by a certain M. Gautin of the Paris *Sûreté*! Then he pulled himself together, deliberately put an arm about Lucille's seductive figure and moved with her on to the dance floor.

Now it was Sylvia's turn to see Johnny. She stopped laughing and dancing and gripped Henri's arm convulsively. She felt she would fall down with astonishment. Her cheeks flamed.

'*Johnny!*' she gasped. 'Good heavens above — *it's Johnny!* But I don't understand . . . what is he doing here and *with your sister!*'

'My sister!' repeated Henri sharply. He followed Sylvia's gaze. Then it was his turn to stare. That Lucille should have dared follow him here instead of returning to Paris as he had ordered, amazed and angered him. And how the devil indeed had she come to join up with Sylvia's young English doctor? Henri's sure instinct warned him that there was something peculiar about this whole affair. With difficulty he controlled his violent temper. The evening with Sylvia had been a great success, but *now* — this damnable interruption!

'I must speak to Johnny' — began Sylvia, and darted through the crowd toward him. Her pulses were jerking uncomfortably. What he was doing with Lucille, to whom they had said good-bye in Dijon, she could not begin to think. The whole thing was a complete mystery.

Johnny watched the slim figure in blue lace approach. He steeled himself for what was coming. But he wished he had never met M. Gautin and never been drawn into this affair. On the other hand, if he could pull it off — and it looked as though he was not on the heels of success — it would be an achievement, and there might be more than that in it: a reward in the shape of that money he needed so badly.

He was the first to speak:

'Why, *hullo*, Silver,' he said in a casual voice. 'Fancy us all running into each other like this! Of course your mother told me you and Kay were heading for the South. I came over with Bob Blunt, you know. By the way, we passed through Orange and saw the Cadillac. Bad show! You girls had a lucky escape.'

She stared at him speechlessly. How could he behave as though they had never meant anything more to each other than *this*. As though this chance meeting — so far from England and home — was of no account?

Henri and Lucille drew apart from the other two. They were sizing each other up warily, both smiling, both ice-cold, full of hate and suspicion.

'How pleasant for you, my dear, to have found new friends to bring you along,' he said.

'Yes, am I not lucky, *mon cher Henri* — and you, too, deserve my congratulations,' she replied, but in an undertone rapidly, in their own language, she added: 'Which is it you are after — the girl or the *emeralds*?'

Under pretext of dropping a kiss on her cheek he hissed against her ear:

'Be quiet! It is my affair and no longer yours. Be careful what you say to your doctor. If you give away anything you will pay for it for the rest of your life!'

She moved back from him uneasily. She was still afraid of Henri.

'I shall say nothing. But I also warn *you, mon cher* — do not give *me* away, or else — ' She broke off, shrugging her shoulders.

And while these two threatened each other, Sylvia and Johnny exchanged a few brief words. Her first inclination had been to throw herself into his arms, wild with joy. But he put a speedy end to that.

'You've soon found yourself a consoler,' he observed bitterly.

She, pale and angry, answered.

'You have no right to insinuate any such thing.'

'Facts speak for themselves,' he said, 'but why should it concern me? Only I advise you not to believe everything you hear from your glamorous M. Chausseur. He may not be all he appears.'

'You know nothing about him. Anyhow — how did *you* meet Mlle Chausseur?'

'In Dijon. Bob and I heard that you girls had been there and we went to the Château to look you up.'

'Thanks,' said Sylvia with a short laugh. 'You should have saved yourself the trouble. And I thought you were so hard up' — she added, with a bitterness to match his — 'and that was why we couldn't get married. It isn't cheap in France, is it?' She laughed again. She was trembling. And all he could do was to stand and glower down at her, yet what he really wanted to do was to pick her up in his arms and say:

'You little fool! I came over to find *you* because I love you!'

And almost he said it. But Henri Chausseur came forward and put an arm through Sylvia's in a proprietary fashion that made Johnny draw back again.

'*Eh bien!*' said Henri. 'Now we have all said 'hullo', shall we continue with our dancing?'

Sylvia hesitated. The first breathless excitement of seeing Johnny — of meeting him here — was over. And things between her and Johnny were all over — for the second time.

'See you at the hotel tomorrow morning,' Johnny drawled in the same infuriating, casual way.

She turned to Henri:

'Please take me back to the hotel!' she said, and was on the verge of tears.

10

Kay Byrne's vitality never flagged for long. The morning after her arrival at the *Roi René* she was up and doing again — back to her usual state of glorious good health. The arm was still in a sling but, nothing daunted, she rose early, flung open the *jalousies* and let a stream of warm sunshine into the big bedroom which she shared with Sylvia. Then she woke Sylvia. She delivered a lecture to the younger girl while they drank their coffee.

Kay had been awake when her cousin got home last night, and having heard all about the arrival of Johnny with Bob Blunt and Lucille, voiced her opinions with her usual logic and good sense.

'If you take my advice you'll quit shedding tears over a fellow who first of all says he doesn't want to marry you because he hasn't any money, then takes his fifty pounds of currency and trails down to the South just in order to have a good time. I don't say I'm crazy about Henri Chausseur, but he's dead nuts about you and couldn't be nicer to both of us. Let your Johnny get on with his life in his own way. Why worry?'

Sylvia listened to this in stark silence. She hadn't really felt quite herself since the accident in the Cadillac, and the shock of the encounter with Johnny last night was the finishing touch. She had wept bleakly into her pillow, wishing she had been born as practical and sensible as Cousin Kay. But she was just the opposite — far too sentimental, and she did love Johnny. But she knew that every word Kay said was right, and the more she thought about Johnny's new interest in Lucille, the more bitter she felt. The hardening-up process was slow with Sylvia. But at the end of Kay's lecture she decided to take the good advice offered. She wouldn't look in Johnny's direction ever again, and she would fortify herself against any further humiliation by letting him see that she was perfectly satisfied with her new 'boy-friend'. Anyhow, Henri *was* wonderful. She was quite sure that if there had never been a Johnny in her life she would have thought the French art collector the most wonderful companion in the world.

Doggedly Sylvia dressed and packed. As she went downstairs she wondered that Johnny had even bothered to go to the *Château des Pines* to see her. Perhaps it was a sign that he didn't care that he should want a casual renewal of what had once been an intense devotion between them. And that he should spend money and time down here in the South in the company of an exotic Parisienne who was a most unsuitable companion for a struggling doctor, didn't make sense.

On her way downstairs as she passed one of the bedrooms, the door opened cautiously and revealed Lucille, looking like a film star in a white, silky dressing-gown, dark hair tied up in a chiffon scarf. Lucille beckoned her in.

'Sylvia — come and talk to me. You are just the one I want to see.'

Sylvia had no wish to go into Lucille's room but could hardly refuse. In here there was a confusion of lovely clothes, and the atmosphere reeked of her perfume. Lucille offered Sylvia a cigarette then did all the talking, mainly about 'Johnee' (every time she said the name it wrenched Sylvia's heart) — it was 'Johnee is so handsome' and 'Johnee is so sweet' and 'How lucky Johnee came on this route with his friend and stopped at Dijon and met her, and of course (here Lucille gave an arch glance at Sylvia through her lashes) 'Brother Henri is so happy to have met Sylvia, and we can all have a splendid time in Monte Carlo.'

Sylvia suffered this torrent of words from Lucille only for a short time, then rose and announced that she needed some fresh air. Lucille, watching her closely, added with apparent nonchalance:

'*Chérie* — do you remember the wonderful, splendid cream I bought from you for the sunburn? I have used *all* — but *all* — I suppose you have no more?'

'I had another tube,' said Sylvia rather curtly — she did not like Lucille and found it difficult to disguise the fact — 'but it burst and there were bits of glass in it so I threw it away last night.'

Lucille shuddered as though someone had struck her a physical blow. Her fixed smile remained, but a trifle weakly she said:

'You threw it — where?'

Sylvia stared.

'Into my waste-paper basket, of course.'

She walked out of the room. Lucille stood with her fingertips pressed against her mouth. Wave after wave of hysterical mirth shook her. *Bits of glass!* The emeralds — Sylvia had flung two million francs' worth of emeralds into her waste-paper basket. *Bon Dieu!*

Lucille's brain worked swiftly. Here was a chance to double-cross Henri and get away with the jewels — and with the *petit docteur*. The big blond Johnee who might marry her and take her back to London. Respectably married, and with a British passport behind her, there was no knowing what she might not be able to do in the future. She could outwit Henri at his own game. As a husband, Johnee would make such a stalwart screen.

Lucille dressed. She made sure that both the English girls were downstairs, then found her way to their bedroom. A quick look inside and her heart sank. The waste-paper basket was empty and the beds stripped. The *femme de chambre* had already been busy. Lucille sent for her. She put a crisp note into the girl's hand.

'There is something in that waste-paper basket that I want,' she said. 'You will say nothing to anybody but you will bring me the contents from the bin into which you have thrown the rubbish.'

The girl began to protest. 'But there was nothing, *Madame, rien*, only — '

Lucille interrupted and her magnificent eyes narrowed.

'All the same, you will show me what you emptied from the basket,' she said, and dangled another note in front of the girl.

It was only a matter of minutes before a dustpan full of the 'rubbish' was brought to *Madame*. Eagerly, and without feeling squeamish, Lucille's long pointed nails rummaged, then fastened eagerly over a messy-looking tube of cream wrapped in a face tissue. Her heart beat fast as she took the treasure along to her own room. With a hairpin she extracted several pieces of 'broken glass'. Her pulses thrilled with excitement. Laughter bubbled in her throat. All there, the precious emeralds! *Henri would never get them now!*

She extracted the gems, cleaned each one and dropped them into a handkerchief which she put into her white nylon bag which had huge silver studs.

164

Faultlessly dressed as usual, Lucille went downstairs and found Johnny on the terrace. He was smoking a pipe in the sunshine, and regarding a *Figaro* with an expression of boredom. Bob Blunt was sitting at a table engaged in an animated conversation with Kay, whom he had met for the first time. They appeared to enjoy what they were saying to each other. Bob was doing a great deal of laughing.

'*Bonjour, Johnee.* Where is the leetle Sylvia?' asked Lucille sweetly.

'Strolling in the garden with your brother.' was Johnny's brusque reply.

'Ah!' sighed Lucille, 'it is *romantique.* The birds are singing. The sun is warm and the sea in Monte Carlo will be blue — oh, so blue! Let us hurry down there, Johnee!'

He eyed her a trifle cautiously. If she knew how little she attracted him, he thought, and how furiously, *damnably,* jealous he was of that French fellow out there in the orangery with Sylvia, Henri — with all his culture and suavity, and the way he spread perpetual cloaks for Sylvia to walk upon — Lucille wouldn't like it much! But he still had to remember the bargain that he had struck with M. Gautin. So when Lucille suggested that they should set off for Monte Carlo without wasting the day in Aix, he fell in with her suggestion.

Bob wasn't quite so ready. He had found the tall, handsome Australian girl a very strong attraction. They were two magnificent specimens of humanity who had appealed to each other at first meeting. Here at last, in Kay's estimation, was a man who could pick her up and carry her off in the good old cave-man style, if he so wanted. And somebody who looked upon life in much the same way as she did — just a vast joke to be much enjoyed.

Bob would have much preferred Kay as his passenger, but could scarcely say so . . . except to Kay herself. She told him that anyhow she couldn't possibly go on with him in the van and leave Sylvia and Henri to themselves.

'Oh, well — it's no way from here to Monte' — said Bob — '150 kilometres at most. We'll make that this morning. Let's all get going. Does anybody know where to stay?'

Lucille pricked up her ears. *She* knew a charming little hotel not far from the sea, she said, which wouldn't be too expensive for the *pauvres anglaises* — the *Hôtel Verlaine*. The proprietor was a friend of hers, and he would give them good rooms and the food was *par excellence*! Did they like shellfish? They could get the most superb *bouillabaise* at the *Verlaine*.

Nobody listened much to Lucille's chatter, but it was agreed they should try the *Hôtel Verlaine*. Then Johnny saw Sylvia's small figure coming toward the hotel, her hand through Henri Chausseur's arm. His lips tightened. He said to Bob:

'Let's get going.'

Bob grinned at Kay.

'So long! Meet me in Monte Carlo, honey!'

'My Colonial oath on that,' said Kay, and hadn't felt better since she was last in Sydney.

Sylvia and her escort joined the group. She had determined to be very strong-minded, so when her eyes met Johnny's she remained cool and casual. They exchanged the most formal of greetings and she did not appear concerned when Johnny announced that they were 'pushing off'.

'We'll be following you,' she said. '*Aur revoir*. See you in Monte some time, Johnny.'

'That you will, Silver, my sweet,' he muttered, but nobody heard the words.

And Lucille patted her white bag and gave her ex-lover the most ravishing smile. *Wouldn't* dear Henri like to know what was in that bag!

Henri was, as always, being charming and attentive, but Sylvia's spirits fell to zero as she watched the little green van move off with the smiling Lucille enthroned on the front seat between the two men. *Oh, damn, damn!* she thought. *Why should this ever have happened? Oh, Johnny, how could you be so faithless? Why did you come here to torment me, when the only reason I came here at all was to try and forget you?*

Blunt's van proceeded at a moderate pace through the wooded countryside, and gradually climbed the splendid Esterel Mountains. They were well on their way now to the *Côte d'Azur*. At one o'clock they had reached Fréjus and stopped for lunch. It was during the coffee that Lucille for one unguarded moment left her precious bag on the table and Johnny picked it up.

'You do have such striking-looking things, Lucille. Is this the *dernier cri* in Paris?' he observed.

She made a sharp movement toward the bag and he was quick to see her expression and drew a natural conclusion. Deliberately he unfastened the clasp.

'Is it nice inside?' he asked, then let it

drop. The contents scattered on the floor. Immediately Johnny went down on one knee and began to pick things up, apologizing profusely. Lucille, white under her rouge, knelt down beside him and made a grab at the powder compact, comb, rouge, money — and a little pile of green stones wrapped in a chiffon handkerchief. Johnny saw those stones. His heart missed a beat but he made no comment. As Lucille bundled everything back into her bag he again apologized for his clumsiness and began to talk about something else. She saw no need for alarm. Even if the emeralds had been placed one by one in front of Dr Garland, he would not know what they were, she reflected. But she must find a better hiding place than her bag once she got to Monte. Knowing the trouble Rex Harris had already had, she was sure she would not be able to get them through the Customs if she should try to take them back to England.

But there was one friend in Monte

whom she particularly wished to see
— the owner of the *Hôtel Verlaine*.
Paul Jerez was half Spanish. He had
done one or two odd jobs for Henri,
who had made the mistake of being
unnecessarily disagreeable to him. In
consequence Jerez disliked Henri but
had, after the manner of Spaniards, a
very soft spot for beautiful women.
Lucille was quite sure that he would
help her dispose of the emeralds, and in
the safest possible manner, without
involving the old gang; taking, of
course, a rake-off for himself.

Lucille was in the highest spirits
when the little green van left the wild
desolate scene of the Alps far behind,
and passing through La Bocca came to
the radiant coast — and Cannes.

Lucille gazed blissfully at the Croi-
sette, and at the blue-glass waters of
the Mediterranean. She murmured to
Johnny:

'Let us be veree happee here — *toi et
moi!*'

Johnny, not because he felt amorous

but because he was so interested in the contents of that white, shiny bag of hers, slipped an arm around her waist. She sighed and leaned her head against his shoulder. Bob glanced at them, raising his brows. He would give up trying to understand people but he had *thought* old Johnny wanted to get down South because of his girl-friend, Silver. Hell take it — he was behaving a bit odd to say the least, even though a chap might be forgiven when a woman of Lucille's allure made a dead set at him. And of course young Silver, herself, was pretty tied up with that French art dealer. One couldn't altogether blame Johnny.

Bob pulled the van up in front of the famous Blue Bar. He was exhilarated by the sight of the sparkling water, the striped umbrellas, the brown bodies lying on the beach, the white Casino, the vivid flowers. All the brilliance and beauty and excitement of the French Riviera.

But when they had parked the van,

Johnny excused himself and left the other two alone for a few moments. He had an important telegram which he must send, he said, before he could enjoy his drink.

Standing his turn in the queue at the *Poste*, Johnny smiled a trifle grimly at what he had written. The wire was addressed to *M. Pierre Gautin, Paris Sûreté*, and the message seemed innocent enough — it was, after all, only what everybody else had been saying today — but it would convey quite a different meaning to the Inspector. It said:

Meet me in Monte Carlo. And was signed with Johnny's initials 'J. G.'.

About an hour after Blunt's van left the *Roi René*, Henri Chausseur's black Citröen also moved swiftly over that same route, heading for Fréjus.

The sun was higher now and the morning beginning to be really hot.

Kay lolled in the spacious back seat, her long legs out-stretched, her bruised arm resting on a cushion, and her mind set on dinner tonight in Monte Carlo with Bob Blunt.

Sylvia, looking rather pale and subdued, occupied the front beside Henri, doing her best to reply with animation to what he was saying. He was religiously pointing out to her all the places and buildings of interest which they passed and had just begun to tell her about a thirteenth-century Gothic church which they came upon soon after leaving Aix-en-Provence, when she broke in suddenly with a single sentence that made him stop talking. He paid the greatest attention to her.

She rubbed one smooth young shoulder and complained of sunburn.

'It was such a nuisance I had to throw away my Cool-creem, Kay,' she said.

'Why did you have to throw it away?' asked Henri sharply. He automatically slowed down. *She had thrown it away!* That infernally elusive tube which he had been so certain was still in her possession. *Bon Dieu!* Here was a nice kettle of fish. He waited in agony for her next words. They confirmed his worst suspicions. The tube had burst and was full of bits of glass, she said innocently, and she had thrown it into her waste-paper basket last night.

Like Lucille, Henri twitched at the mere mention of the *broken glass*. He said:

'Wouldn't you like to go back for it?'

She turned her wide, limpid gaze on him, smiling.

'I wouldn't find it, even if we went back. Do you know, your sister is so mad about that stuff she actually got our *femme de chambre* to fish the messy old tube out of the dustbin, and took it off. The *femme de chambre* told me just as I was leaving. She thought it was so extraordinary.'

'Mlle Lucille certainly is nuts about Cool-creem,' put in Kay from the back. 'They ought to give her a rake-off for advertisement. And you'd have thought something much better could be bought in Paris.'

'My sister can be as Sylvia says — *extraordinary*' said Henri between his teeth; and stepped so suddenly on the accelerator that the black Citröen shot forward jerkily. His darkly tanned face was a mask, but those pale blue eyes of his were brilliant with rage. *So!* Lucille had decided to double-cross him, had she? It was *she* who had those little pieces of 'green glass' tucked away in *her* bag at this very moment, and he had no doubt whatsoever that she intended to act the innocent and get away with the haul before he could interfere.

Henri's brain twisted and turned like a serpent. But he resumed his pleasant descriptions of places of interest as they drove along. And now he, like Johnny in Cannes, decided that it was imperative that he should stop at the *Poste*. There, he put a long-distance call through to Dijon, to the *Château des Pines*. A cautious voice answered in bad French.

Henri recognized the voice and spoke in English.

'So, you've got there at last, have you, Rex?'

'Yes, Henri, and look here, I don't understand — '

'You are not required to understand,' broke in Henri. 'I know everything and I wish you to say nothing. Kindly tell Marcel my instructions are that he shuts down the house, tells everybody that I am going to England on a holiday, and returns to Paris to wait my next move. I wish *you* to hire a car and drive straight down South and meet me in Monte Carlo.'

A gasp from Rex Harris.

'You know my mother's house,' added Henri, 'you will come straight there.'

'Okay,' from Rex.

'Hold on,' said Henri. A sudden rather pleasing thought had struck him. Two memories in fact: one of an Alsatian laying his muzzle on the shoulder of a fair young girl; the other of that same dog with teeth bared, springing out from under a desk upon an ashen-faced, cowering Lucille.

He spoke again.

'And just one thing more, *mon cher* Rex. You will bring Setti with you. Marcel can put him on the lead. He will sit quite happily in the back of the car. He enjoys travelling. And I have another treat in store for him — *also in Monte Carlo*!'

11

Five o'clock in the afternoon in Monte Carlo.

A sea as blue as the crudest colours splashed by an artist reflecting the cobalt sky. White-sailed boats cutting through the water. The glittering white and gilt of the Casino buildings. The dark green of the exotic palm trees. All the elegance of the *Côte d'Azur*; luxury hotels, brilliant flowers banked in their star-shaped beds; shuttered villas in lovely gardens dreaming over the bay. Flags flying on the millionaires' yachts moored in the harbours.

Monte Carlo, playground of the rich, and in the gambling room the ceaseless turn of the roulette wheel and the click of the little ivory ball, spinning in the hot, smoke-filled *salles des Jeux*.

Out of the *Hôtel Verlaine*, a villa with rose-coloured walls and pale-green shutters, came four people, carrying bathing suits and towels. Sylvia and Kay, followed by Johnny and Bob, who were both anxious, they said, to acquire an all-over tan. Kay's arm was so much improved that she had dropped the sling. She was sure a swift bathe in the salt, sparkling water would put her quite right. Sylvia, too, looked and felt better. But this party had been none of her making. She had, in fact, tried to get out of it. But Kay had been rather cunning. The Australian girl was quite sure in her own mind that this misunderstanding between her cousin and the young doctor was a lot of nonsense, and the more she saw of Henri Chausseur the more she distrusted him. She was determined to break it up and bring Sylvia and Johnny together again. She said:

'Let's get rid of the two Frenchies and have an all-British swimming party. Come along — and be natural.'

So Sylvia had come with them and was laughing and talking to Johnny just as though they had never parted and never reached such a deadlock. She thought without pleasure of last night. It should have been a wonderful evening, spent in the gay, glittering Casino and she had had what should have been a wonderful time with Henri.

But Johnny had not been there. Lucille hadn't wanted to go to the Casino with the others, and he had seemed quite willing to take her off to her favourite restaurant, driving out to the *Château de Madrid*, which was high on the cliffs overlooking Villefranche. Sylvia had watched them depart and tried to play up to Henri, even to respond when he attempted to make love to her. But one kiss and she had torn herself away, knowing that she could never love him. He, undaunted, had soothed her and said:

'I can wait — forever if necessary. I adore you. One day you will love me.'

So here they were today — all bent on having a jolly time! But no Lucille. She had announced that she wanted to stay behind at the hotel and take a siesta. But Johnny, before leaving, had watched her walking in the garden with her old friend, the black-haired, black-eyed proprietor, Paul Jerez who had been away on business when they arrived yesterday.

Johnny knew perfectly well what the 'huddle' was about, but had decided to let them get on with their conference. He was now going to wait for Gautin to arrive before he made his next move. Meanwhile, he was willing to let Lucille have her head, and thankful to get away from her cloying, over-amorous approach for a while.

She would join her Johnee on the beach, she had said sweetly, in a *ravissante Bikini* which would display to him her luscious limbs. Henri, who was staying with his mother, also intended to join them after lunch. When, yesterday, Sylvia had expressed surprise that his 'sister' should not be with her mother and brother, Henri had given the deadliest smile.

'She will come — later on,' he had said. 'She and our mother do not — shall we say — *get on*. But I will prepare the way for a nice little reconciliation.'

Down on the *plage* the 'British party' undressed in the scorching sun and waded into the warm water. Johnny looked through dark glasses at Sylvia and felt all the old tenderness for her surge into his heart. What a little darling she was — his Silver — his pocket Venus. Her ivory, slim body was full of nymph-like grace in a pale blue silk swimsuit with gilt hair tied up in a pale blue scarf. She was enchanting, and he wished that he could explain everything to her; oh, darn it! But this afternoon Gautin should be here and then all this nonsense would be over. He could tell his Silver why he had behaved with such apparent indifference.

Suddenly, overcome, he splashed through the water toward her, and called to her urgently:

'Silver!'

She saw the radiant sky tremble above her, but she gave him a long, reproachful look.

'Oh, hello — oughn't you to have waited to bring Lucille down?' she asked coldly.

Johnny drew breath.

'Maybe you're right,' he said, and dived into the water, forgetting he had his own glasses on, then spent an embarrassing moment standing on his head trying to find them.

The salt of Sylvia's stinging tears mingled with the salt of the blue Mediterranean water. But she gasped in a high-pitched voice:

'Oh, *gorgeous*! — what a lovely life! Think, it's probably cold and *raining* back home.'

In a narrow, shabby-looking villa in *La Condamine* — which bore the name *La Retour* — Henri Chausseur sat in the small salon talking with his mother.

She was blind, and she was very old. She was the one being on earth whom he had ever truly loved. Perhaps the only one who knew nothing of his vices and who believed him to be perfect. Once he had lived decently, with his respectable parents, in Grasse.

His father worked in a perfume factory. The young Henri was spoilt from birth by *Madame* Chausseur. He had always exerted a strange, mesmeric influence over women.

An uncle, better off than M. Chausseur, had paid for the boy to go to a good school. The education had, perhaps, been his ruin. Later, a certain Frenchwoman of means, older than himself, had fallen in love with the handsome youth, taken him to Paris and introduced him to the world of art and antiques; also to a special world peopled with successful criminals. In both these worlds Henri proved an apt pupil. His father had died, since when Henri had taken care of his mother. For the last twenty years she had been totally blind and lived here in the villa her son had bought for her. He took cover here in *La Retour* from time to time, for it was the last place in which one might anticipate finding a man of his type.

Henri Chausseur's whole face altered as he spoke now with his mother, and lost all its rapaciousness. Dreamily he looked around the familiar salon, stiffly furnished in the ornate French style which she had always loved. There was no one in the house except old Helène, the servant, who looked after her.

'All is well with you, my son?' she asked.

'Yes,' he said, 'except that at the moment I am interested in a big deal and there are those who are trying to cheat me. While I am staying with you here this time, *Maman*, I wish you and not Helène to answer the door bell. You will tell all callers that your invalid son lives with you and is laid up and must see no one. There are those who wish to find me, but I do not wish them to trouble me. There is only one you may admit — my English friend, Mr Harris, who will arrive any moment now.'

Mme Chausseur nodded. It pleased her to be able to help her son in his business, and she had very often in the past kept her poor, tired boy away from those who endeavoured to worry him. He needed a rest when he came to *La Retour*.

Then she asked the question that she had been asking him for the past ten years.

'Is there still no one whom you wish to marry, my son?'

This time he laid a hand on her knee and said:

'Yes. An English girl, fairer than an angel and purer than the snow on the Alps. I shall bring her to you, perhaps tomorrow. You shall touch her face and judge her beauty and goodness with your own hands. She perhaps will become your daughter-in-law.'

The old lady was pleased and excited. She had long since wanted Henri to marry and have children of his own.

Now he grew restless. He thought of Lucille up at the *Hôtel Verlaine* and of what she had done to him. He knew exactly what she was playing at. Did she think that she and Paul Jerez could get away with it? Soon it would be time for him to deal with her.

But in the hotel gardens, Lucille had come to a very amicable arrangement with Paul Jerez. Just for a moment she had allowed him to hold her in his arms and drink the wine of madness from her voluptuous mouth. Then said:

'If you will help me, I will return to you. We neither of us need work for Henri Chausseur again.'

He must put the emeralds in the hotel safe, and dispose of them one by one in suitable places. She, meanwhile, with perhaps one or two of them on her, would go to London with her new English friends and stay there, where Henri could not get at her. When Paul thought it safe to send for her, she would come.

'What is he planning down there at

La Retour?' Jerez asked fearfully.

Lucille replied:

'He wants the emeralds, but he will not find them. He thinks Sylvia has them still. As for his plans, I neither know nor care, except that he wishes to marry the stupid English girl. But that is of no interest to me.'

'You love *me*?'

'*De tout coeur!*' she answered, and then, humming a little tune, watched him lock the emeralds in his safe and knew that she need not be afraid to trust the poor, besotted fellow. She could twist him round one finger. So she left him and went off to join Johnny on the beach. She had left him alone long enough with the 'little English idiot'. Now she must turn the big guns upon him and seal her victory.

She reached the others just as they were coming out of the water. Attaching herself to Johnny, she monopolized the conversation for the rest of the time they were there. By six o'clock the sun began to sink and the party agreed that it was time to break up and go home.

Sylvia, whatever weakness had temporarily seized her while she was swimming with Johnny, hardened up again as she watched the French girl so flagrantly coquetting with him. And Johnny — so she imagined — responded with the sort of sidelong ardent glance that he used to reserve for *her*.

As they all walked through the Casino gardens, she could not resist being what she termed a little 'witchy'.

'Not been to see your mother yet, Lucille?'

Lucille had to blink a moment to remember who her mother was. Then, uttering a tinkling laugh, she jangled the eight bracelets which made an accompanying concert on her smooth bare arm.

'*Ooh! la, la!* I leave her to my dear brother. They adore each other — but I — I am the poor little unwanted one. Don't you think that's sad, to be unwanted, *mon petit docteur*?'

She turned to Johnny. He mumbled an answer. He was not concentrating on what she said. His eye was on his wrist-watch, and he was considering the time it would take M. Gautin to reach Monte Carlo.

Bob Blunt gave his tremendous laugh and said to Kay:

'What about you, are you a little unwanted one, darling? Would you like to take an aperitif with me? I like you with your hair plastered to your head. You look like a bronze figure of health and strength!'

'Bronze figure yourself!' she jeered at him.

And linking arms they walked side by side into the Casino, cigarettes between their lips, towels over their shoulders, looking in truth as though they had been hewn from bronze . . . god and goddess of Golden Youth.

Sylvia felt suddenly sick.

Mon petit docteur. Lucille's little doctor indeed! How she loathed the woman! Sylvia was glad to see Henri's debonair figure approaching them. He had changed into a white sharkskin suit and wore a buttonhole. He had a panama hat on the side of his head, which he raised as he sighted the little party. He kissed Sylvia's hand, but his strange blue eyes rested on Lucille, who returned his gaze boldly if a trifle uneasily.

'Alas! I am too late to bathe with you all, *mes enfants*,' he said.

'Won't you join us now?' asked Sylvia.

He murmured an excuse and continued to look at Lucille.

'*Maman* is asking for you,' he said in a silky voice.

She bit her lip.

'Tomorrow, perhaps —' she began.

But Henri put an arm through hers and said quite lightly:

'I think, *ma chère*, it would cheer her up if you would come and see her now. The Citröen is outside, and we shall drive to *La Retour* together. You shall chat with *Maman* awhile and then I shall return you to your friends.'

Suddenly Lucille felt cold. She recognized the pressure of Henri's thin fingers gripping her arm, and that steely line of lips. His smile had a knife edge. She was suddenly afraid. *What did he know?* What could he have found out? Why did he want her to go to *La Retour?* In all the years of intimacy, he had never once allowed her inside the villa; she had never met his mother.

She tried to break away from him, but there was no refusing Henri this time.

Johnny and Sylvia stood watching the French girl drive away in the Citröen beside her handsome 'brother'. Sylvia felt nervous and ill at ease now that she was alone for the first time with Johnny.

'Well?' she began.

'If you'll excuse me,' said Johnny, as though something was sticking in his throat, 'can I leave you to find Kay and Bob in the Casino? I have an important engagement.'

Scarlet with chagrin, in pain and

bewilderment, Sylvia stood staring after Johnny as his tall figure strode away. So it was like *that*! He was so much infatuated with Lucille that he could not bear to be left alone with *her* for one moment. She could not know, of course, that he had just recognized the familiar figure of M. Gautin strolling across the terrace overlooking the Casino gardens. And that this was where he *had* to leave Sylvia alone, even though he offended her bitterly.

In the car, climbing the hill to *La Retour*, Lucille said shrilly:

'What do you want with me? You told me to get out when I was at the Château. It is my business if I choose to make new friends now — isn't it?'

He gave a cynical laugh.

'We can both make new friends, Lucille, but that is no reason for betraying our old ones.'

Now she blanched. Pearls of sweat formed on her forehead. *She knew that he knew about the emeralds.*

'Let me out of the car,' she said

wildly. 'I don't trust you!'

'I have never trusted *you*,' he said, and added softly, 'nor Paul Jerez.'

'I don't know what you mean —' she began.

He swung the powerful car round a bend in the drive and pulled up in a cloud of dust in front of the shuttered villa. Another car was there; one that had just brought Rex Harris and Setti, the Alsatian, from Dijon to *La Retour*.

Through her teeth, Lucille said:

'You won't dare touch me. Johnny will come and look for me.'

'Johnny can have you when I've finished with you,' Henri said pleasantly, 'and no doubt the emeralds are quite safe in Paul's hands. I will call and collect them later tonight.'

Lucille gasped like a floundering fish.

'*Mon Dieu!*' she said, and put a hand to her throat.

She had no time to scream and she would not have been heard anyway. On this quiet golden morning, there was nobody in this vicinity. The garden drowsed in the sun. The eucalyptus trees, and the oleanders, shed a sweet perfume. And for the first time in her life Lucille entered the portals of *La Retour*. Through a chink in the shutters Rex Harris signalled to Henri; nodding his head. Henri knew then that his mother and Helène had been taken for a drive and that nobody else was there.

Lucille began to whimper; she would get the emeralds back — she would give them to him, of course — she had never meant to steal — only to scare him into thinking they were lost beyond recall because she was jealous — jealous of Sylvia.

Henri made no comment on what she said. He drew her across the hall and pointed to a closed, carved oaken door.

'In there you will find a friend waiting for you,' he said.

And he pushed her violently, so that she almost fell into the room. His voice followed:

'*A l'attaque, mon brave!*'

Lucille had no time to think. But in a split second of lunatic fear she saw her old enemy, Setti, the Alsatian, spring at her from across the room. She felt the hot breath of the dog against her cheek and the agonizing pain of teeth in her throat. Then in a whirl of agony and terror she went down screaming as those sharp fangs lacerated the beautiful, terror-stricken face.

12

In an unobtrusive café not far from the Casino, Johnny Garland sat eating a *tournedos* in the company of M. Gautin. They were drinking a light white wine. Johnny swallowed his somewhat feverishly, for his mind was in a turmoil. Although interested in all M. Gautin was saying, his mind kept reverting to the memory of Sylvia and that shocked look in her eyes when he so abruptly left her. She must think him unpardonably rude and unkind. But this was the 'last lap'. He would thank his stars when the *Sûreté* had finished with him.

M. Gautin, noisily chewing his steak and with a smug, pleased look on his saturnine countenance, said:

'Assuredly, my dear young man, you have been of the greatest help to us and that help shall not go unrewarded.'

'Well, I only hope I don't find myself in the soup as far as my girl-friend is concerned,' muttered Johnny.

'You will be able to explain to her this evening.'

'It'll want some explaining!'

M. Gautin signalled to the waiter and ordered *deux cafés et deux fines maison.* He was partial to a good cognac and he thought the young English doctor needed something stronger than the *Sauterne.*

'You will be able to tell the young lady,' he said, 'that once we knew the circumstances in Paris, and being aware of the wily habits of these jewel thieves, whom we have suspected for some time but have never been able to pin down, we thought it best to enlist the help of the young Englishman who has, shall we say, a very innocent look!'

'Let us trust that my girl-friend believes in my innocence,' Johnny grunted, and wondered just what Silver was saying about him at that moment to Kay. 'And now what are your plans for the final round-up?' he added.

Gautin pursed his lips. So far, things had gone well. It had been wonderful luck securing the English doctor's help as a kind of decoy and amateur detective. And he had done it so well. Chausseur and his confederates had fallen into the trap. They had felt so safe in the company of Johnny Garland and a couple of hitch-hikers. And Gautin had been quite certain that one of them would slip up sooner or later; that the emeralds would turn up. Yes, the *jeune docteur* had been most capable and shown a quick wit which made him a worthy ally. And now they all knew that the emeralds were in the safe at the *Hôtel Verlaine*. But M. Gautin did not intend to raid the hotel immediately. First he wanted to get the master mind of the gang to betray himself. The charming and much-respected art connoisseur of Dijon and his ex-mistress, Lucille Renard, must behave in such a fashion that M. Gautin could make an arrest. After this he could keep them firmly behind bars for the next few years. Already the hue and cry in England after the man who had so mercilessly assaulted the diamond merchant in Hatton Garden had been brought to a successful conclusion. A gentleman named 'Flick' and his girl-friend were both in prison awaiting trial. There were others to follow, but tonight, Gautin reflected cheerfully, the haul would be magnificent, and the big reward for the emeralds which the English insurance company had offered would go into the pockets of Dr John Garland. Very nice, too, for a man who had need of this nest egg as he wanted to get married.

'We shall go cautiously, and it will be best if I and my colleagues still do not present ourselves in person either at the *Hôtel Verlaine* or *La Retour* just for the moment,' explained Gautin. 'Now my suggestion is this —'

Sipping his cognac he leaned across the table and voiced his plans.

Johnny thought:

'Hold on, Silver! Don't hate me too badly . . . and don't fall any further for Henri Chausseur. I'm on my way to you. Just hold on!'

But unfortunately Sylvia was not able to hear this call from Johnny's heart. She had returned to the *Hôtel Verlaine* not with any intention of bemoaning the fact that Johnny had behaved so atrociously, but bubbling over with anger and indignation. For the rest of that day she listened to Kay's various accounts of Bob and what they were doing and saying, and how that big, handsome boy made her knees knock together every time she saw him, and that she was just the happiest girl who ever left Australia. It was about tea-time when Sylvia, who had been remarkably silent all afternoon, returned to the hotel with her cousin after another session on the beach — this time without Johnny — and said:

'I can't stay here. I suggest that you ask Bob and Johnny to drive you back in their van. I'm going to fly home, even if it costs me all my money. And even if I crash to my doom — it won't matter if I do.'

Kay, who had been living in a world of her own ever since Bob entered it, was shocked by the sight of the stark unhappiness in Sylvia's eyes.

'Honey, what's happened?'

'Everything,' broke in Sylvia. 'I hate Johnny Garland and I don't ever want to see him again, and as he's here in Monte Carlo, I'm getting out of it.'

'But you're mistaken,' said Kay, 'I know from what Bob told me that Johnny is still 'nuts' about you.'

Sylvia gave a theatrical laugh and went upstairs to her room, announcing that she wished to pack her rucksack. Kay followed.

'But what about Henri?'

'I don't want him either. I don't want anybody. I just want to go home.'

'If it's Lucille you're jealous of — I know you needn't be because Bob said Johnny would soon be able to explain everything.'

'He won't be able to explain anything to *me*,' said Sylvia.

At that moment a *femme de chambre* announced that M. Jerez begged to speak to the young ladies. He had, alas, some bad news.

Sylvia and Kay went downstairs. They found Paul Jerez in the empty bar looking grey in the face and wiping the sweat from his forehead. He greeted them in a croaking voice. They only just managed to make out what he was saying. But certainly it was shocking news. The beautiful Mlle Lucille had just been taken by ambulance to a hospital in Cannes. No — not ill — but she had been attacked by a ferocious dog and badly mauled.

Jittering, the Frenchman, who truly loved Lucille, wept into his handkerchief.

'Her beauty!' he sobbed. 'Ah, *Bon Dieu*! That wonderful face — lacerated — scarred for ever. Even in the hands of the finest plastic surgeon, she can never again look the same. She may even die of shock and loss of blood.'

The English girls exchanged glances. They both felt a little sick. Neither of them had liked Lucille. Sylvia in particular had loathed her. But one would not wish a fate like that on one's worst enemy. The hysterical Paul sobbed on.

He had no idea where this episode had taken place. Someone from the hospital had just telephoned. Lucille had recovered consciousness and asked to see him. Of course he was going immediately.

'If we can do anything —' began Sylvia.

'Just pack some clothes and give them to me to take to her,' nodded Paul.

Sylvia frowned perplexedly at her cousin.

'But her brother — Henri — has he been told?'

Paul expressed ignorance on this matter. He was only too well aware of what little interest Henri would take in the ugly fate that had befallen his former mistress. But these English girls still regarded her as Henri's sister, and it was not up to Paul to enlighten them. He must go at once to the bedside of his unfortunate Lucille and assure her that the emeralds would remain safely in his possession.

Sylvia and Kay entered a room that reeked of Lucille's familiar perfume, packed some of her enchanting lingerie and took the suitcase down to M. Jerez. At that moment a young boy came through the flower-filled garden and handed a note to the proprietor. Jerez dropped the bag and tore open the envelope. His tear-streaked face turned a shade more grey. The letter was written in Henri Chausseur's small, fine hand. It said:

It may interest you to know that the accident of which you have been informed by the hospital authorities took place at La Retour. *It is deeply distressing, but I do not think our poor Lucille will ever regain her former glamour. And alas, it* was my own dear *Setti* who attacked my beloved sister . . . [the sister was heavily underlined]. You will tell this to the English ladies if they do not already know. You will also inform Mlle Sylvia that I would be honoured if she would pay me a visit here this afternoon. But in deference to my wishes not to mention one word of the tragedy to my mother from whom we are keeping the bad news on account of her great age.

As for you, my dear Jerez, you have, I believe, a number of green apples which Lucille brought from Dijon. I am particularly partial to the flavour of these and must ask you to bring them here at once. Otherwise I shall be compelled to fetch them, and after my 'sister's' fearful accident I am sure you would not put me to such trouble.

It was signed 'H. C.'.

The two girls, watching Jerez, saw that the letter had a peculiarly unhappy effect on him. He shook visibly. They heard him say: '*Mort de Dieu!*' several times under his breath.

'It isn't more bad news about Mlle Lucille, I hope?' said Sylvia anxiously.

'No,' said Paul in a sepulchral voice. 'But news personally bad for me. And I have a message for you from M. Chausseur.'

He delivered it. It was received by a silent Sylvia. She had meant to leave the *Hôtel Verlaine* this very moment, but of course Henri had been very good to her and he seemed genuinely in love with her. She owed it to him to pay a visit to *La Retour* and commiserate with him on this dreadful thing that had happened to his sister. And of *course* she wouldn't say a word to the poor old mother.

She had yet to learn that the terrible injuries to Lucille were the result of an attack made by that same fine-looking Alsatian that had won her admiration at the *Château des Pines*.

She left Kay at the hotel and walked through the sunshine in the direction of *La Retour* with M. Jerez. Her face was solemn and a little flushed. *His* held a look of deathly fear. And in his pocket lay a perfumed chiffon handkerchief which, mysteriously enough, contained the 'green apples'. For he knew, that the game was up. *Henri knew!* What fate awaited him, Jerez, for having tried to get away with those emeralds for Lucille's sake, remained to be seen. But one thing he did know. It was not the slightest use trying to get away. Henri would find him.

In fact, if he valued his life, this act of surrender was, he knew his only hope of preserving his own good looks.

13

So the final scene was laid within the quiet portals of *La Retour*.

It all began just as soon as Paul Jerez, with Sylvia, who wore a big straw hat, carried white gloves and looked as though she had come to call, rang the bell outside the iron gates of the shabby villa.

Henri appeared. Not the dapper, smiling man who had become well known to Sylvia, but one with a yellowish tinge to his tan and a harassed expression which altered only for a moment as he saw Sylvia.

'I hoped to stop you coming — but when I rang the hotel you had already left,' were his opening words.

'I thought you wished me to call on your mother. I am so horrified about Lucille.'

Henri chewed his lip nervously. The

beauty of this young girl which he had found so disturbing had little effect upon him today. His mind was on other things. Certainly not on 'poor Lucille'. But he had, a moment ago, received a disturbing telephone call from Rex Harris, who had been down in the town this afternoon and who assured him that he had seen that dolt of an English doctor 'Johnee' in the company of Pierre Gautin of the Paris *Sûreté*. It did not seem possible to Henri, even supposing Gautin was in Monte Carlo. (Henri knew, of course, that they were suspicious in Paris.) But what would Gautin want with Dr Garland? Rex, however, was certain, and Henri was a worried man. He said:

'Did you bring the — er — apples?'

Jerez wiped his forehead.

'*Si.*'

'Take them into the house and wait for me. I will deal with you later,' said Henri.

They spoke in French; so rapidly that Sylvia did not understand. As Jerez opened the door, a sleek, smooth body sprang gracefully into the sunshine. Sylvia went down on one knee and opened her arms.

'Oh, it's that darling *Setti*!' she said, suddenly forgetting to be miserable because she was so fond of animals and she thought Henri's Alsatian the *loveliest* dog.

Henri looked at her. For the second time, he felt the pang of a connoisseur who regards something rare and exquisite; this beautiful fair girl — so fearlessly embracing his noble dog, whose tail wagged in appreciation and whose tongue licked her hand. *Bon Dieu!* he thought. And this was the same Setti who this morning had obeyed his command and meted out such frightful punishment to a traitor.

Well — all was over now. No doubt Lucille would 'squeal' At any rate, Monte Carlo had become too hot for Henri. He would take the emeralds, split them up amongst those whom he could trust, and get away from France into Spain by private plane if it were possible.

Sylvia stood up and looked a trifle shyly at the Frenchman.

'I've come to say good-bye,' she murmured. 'I'm not going to stay here as long as I expected.'

Henri sighed and held on to her fingers for a second.

'I also must leave Monte Carlo. But one day soon I shall come to London,' he began.

But that was as far as he got. A black Renault swept up the hill and pulled up in a cloud of dust and grinding of brakes outside *La Retour*. This was the moment for which Pierre Gautin had been waiting. They were all here now.

Sylvia recognized Johnny sitting beside the driver. For a second she prepared a speech which she hoped would flatten him out. But she was never given an opportunity to deliver it.

She saw Henri turn. With an agility worthy of Setti he streaked into the house. Crash went the door. Shutters in the downstairs were hastily jerked together. Gautin, revolver in hand, spat a command in his own language at the two police officers in plain clothes sitting in the back of the Renault. One ran round to the left of the villa, the other to the right. Sylvia began to wonder if she was imagining things. Then Johnny rushed to her, pulled her forcibly through the gate and out of the garden.

'Quick — down!' he commanded in a voice that she had never heard before from Johnny, and she looked up into the square face of a man who sees danger ahead and is enjoying himself. Dazed, she heard him add:

'Right down there . . . behind that hedge, and don't move until you're told!'

'But why —?' began Sylvia, and was indignant to find herself literally hurled on to the grassy bank.

'Don't ask questions now! Lie low! There's going to be some shooting.'

'I don't understand — Johnny!' she

called after him, her face crimson.

'You will soon!' he yelled back at her. 'Your pal Henri Chausseur is one of the most wanted men in France, that's all!'

Now all her blood rose in terror for *him* — forgotten all differences of opinion. She only knew that she loved him.

'Johnny!'

'I love you, Silver, but for the love of Mike keep down behind that hedge,' he entreated, and went back to the front door of *La Retour.* Gautin was shouting.

'Open up, Chausseur! Otherwise we'll break the door down! The place is surrounded. You can't get away!'

A shot broke the lush silence of the golden afternoon, which had that unearthly, ethereal beauty of sunsets on the *Côte d'Azur.* Gautin and Johnny ducked. Another bullet whined. Johnny lay full length on the grass panting. Gautin said irritably:

'He's an *imbecile* to give us this

trouble. If anyone gets hurt he'll go to the guillotine.'

Then the shooting stopped abruptly. The door opened. A man staggered out, holding a hand to his throat. Henri Chausseur, with the livid hue of death on his face and blood on his speckless sharkskin jacket. Gautin ran forward to catch him as he swayed. He gave a feeble, cynical smile.

'It should have been you, my old friend, but Jerez — the traitor — had two bullets in his own automatic . . . the first was for my dog because he mauled Lucille — the second was for *me*. There isn't a third . . . you can go in and get him. You'll be quite safe.'

Sylvia had heard the voices. Disobeying Johnny's command she crawled to the gate and looked through. Then she saw the horrifying sight of the man she had thought an innocent art collector lying there on the sun-warmed grass in a welter of his own blood. He had strength left for only one more speech.

'Need not . . . tell my mother about

this, Gautin . . . She is . . . very deaf . . . she hasn't heard. She need not know.' And then: '*Adieu, petite fleur.*'

The last two words were whispered to Sylvia. His head fell back. The next thing Sylvia knew was that Johnny was leading her towards the car and she was crying against his coat. And he was trying to tell all that had been happening. In a daze she sat holding on to his hand, listening to the explanations. At last she knew that he had accepted the job as the 'outside man', of helping the *Sûreté* to net their prey.

She looked at him with an expression of one who still does not quite understand. Johnny hugged her.

'Okay, darling — I'm quite sure your little mind can't take it all in. Don't worry too much. We've found each other again. That is what matters.'

She nodded, but her thoughts were clearing and she was beginning to see the daylight. It was all very extraordinary and a little shocking to her.

'It's incredible to me that *you* of all

people in the world getting mixed up in a show like this, Johnny.'

'Darling, I assure you I had no intention of being in it until those *Sûreté* chaps got hold of me outside the *Château des Pines*. But they made it sound so tempting. First of all, you know my weakness for reading thrillers. Give me a Cheyney or an Agatha Christie and I've always been a happy man. When I saw an actual chance myself of helping the police track down a couple of dangerous criminals, it was too much for me. And then there was the reward. A pretty big one, darling. More than enough to help us furnish a very nice little cottage somewhere outside Manchester.'

Now Sylvia flushed and her eyes brimmed.

'Oh! So you're really proposing to me — and this time properly, are you, Johnny?'

'I am, darling. And I'm hellishly sorry I caused you so much unhappiness. I've been just as miserable myself.'

'Serve you right, darling.'

'Darling, you're much too beautiful to be spiteful.'

Now she buried her face against his shoulder; the tears were dripping down her cheeks but she was still laughing.

'It's too much — I can't take it. I thought it was all over with us, and to wake up — and find this — oh, Johnny, *Johnny!*'

He kissed the top of her head and gave her his handkerchief.

'Don't cry, Silver, it's going to be all right. I swear I won't make any more fuss. We'll go straight back to England and I'll ask your father in the approved style for the hand of his daughter.'

Sylvia blew her nose.

'I'm quite sure you'll get it, too. Anyhow, nobody can keep us apart now.'

Then she turned her attention to the scene before her.

Two more cars had just pulled up in front of the little villa. Several men in uniform spilled out of the first. A man in plain clothes, and one in check shirt and slacks and beret carrying a couple of cameras followed.

Sylvia shivered.

'Now there's going to be this horrible business of photographing the scene of the capture and us. It will all be in the French press.'

Johnny cursed under his breath.

'I'm afraid we're bound to be dragged into it, darling. I'm sorry. Let them take your photograph quickly, if they must, then I'll take you along to find Kay. You two girls must stick together until I've got through all the formalities and then I'm quite sure Bob will forgive me if we don't stay in Monte Carlo. I'd like to fly home with you. You'd like that, too, wouldn't you?'

She nodded and pressed his hand. Her wet eyes took in the sight of the blue of the sky and the lush green of the trees in the little garden that had sheltered Henri Chausseur's mother;

the oleanders, the exotic bougain-villaea. All the warmth and beauty that was Monte Carlo. But somehow it no longer seemed beautiful to Sylvia. Death and violence and crime were ugly things. And no matter what he had done, it was a horrible thought that Henri, so intelligent, so charming and helpful so recently her companion, lay behind those shutters — *dead*.

Strange to say, she felt even more sorry that Setti had had to die. No matter what he had done to Lucille — it had not been the animal's fault. Henri had trained him to violence and made a criminal of him. But he was still the fine dog who had licked Sylvia's hand and given her such a friendly welcome.

'Oh, it's all *horrible* — let me get away soon,' she said, and began to cry again.

The photographer wearing the beret approached, shouting at them to wait while he took their photographs. When he had finished, M. Gautin came out of the villa and spoke to Johnny.

'We'll be through in a moment or two. Fortunately the old lady is still asleep — deaf as a door-post. We'll find a nurse and get her taken to a home. Obviously she can't stay at *La Retour*. But we'll deal with her as gently as possible.'

Here Sylvia put in a word.

'Yes — the poor old thing — she loved her son. It will be such a ghastly blow to her when she learns the truth.'

'Maybe we can keep it from her and tell her that Chausseur died, say, in a car accident,' suggested Johnny.

Pierre Gautin lit a small black cigar. He chuckled.

'The English are very sentimental — yes?'

Johnny squeezed Sylvia's hand.

'Yes,' he said.

Later Johnny was driving Sylvia down the hill towards her hotel.

'Forget it all now,' he said. 'Don't let it sadden you, darling.'

'Well, I do think it was rather sad,

Johnny. And to think of me figuring in a shooting — well, it just doesn't suit me, does it?'

'No, I admit it would have suited your cousin Kay a lot better. Sorry I dragged you into it, darling.'

'I rather think it was *I* who dragged *you* into it, Johnny. After all, I was the one who had made friends with that unhappy man.'

'And let me tell you I was darned jealous when I saw you dancing with him that night in Aix-en-Provence.'

'What about you and Lucille?'

Johnny stopped the car, turned to Sylvia and gave her a long look.

'Silver, let me tell you here and now — Lucille had lovely legs, who is to deny it? They were poems and she knew it, but she was about the most detestable and infuriating kind of woman alive. Apart from being totally without morals — the 'gangster's moll' complete — she was greedy, sensual, and she deserved what she got, and that's saying something.'

223

Sylvia shivered.

'Yes that's saying something,' she repeated in a whisper.

He drew her closer.

'I'm mad about you, Silver.'

'So am I about you, Johnny.'

Which was none of it very original, but totally satisfying to them both. Then just for one lucid moment, as Sylvia stepped out of the car in front of her hotel, she referred to that momentous adventure which they had shared.

'Imagine — when I threw away that tube of Cool-creem, I threw away two million francs' worth of emeralds!'

Johnny gave a dry laugh.

'You'll have to be more careful in future. You won't get any emeralds once you're married to a struggling doctor, darling. At least, not for some long time!'

We do hope that you have enjoyed reading this large print book.

Did you know that all of our titles are available for purchase?

We publish a wide range of high quality large print books including:
Romances, Mysteries, Classics
General Fiction
Non Fiction and Westerns

Special interest titles available in large print are:
The Little Oxford Dictionary
Music Book, Song Book
Hymn Book, Service Book

Also available from us courtesy of Oxford University Press:
Young Readers' Dictionary
(large print edition)
Young Readers' Thesaurus
(large print edition)

For further information or a free brochure, please contact us at:
Ulverscroft Large Print Books Ltd.,
The Green, Bradgate Road, Anstey,
Leicester, LE7 7FU, England.
Tel: (00 44) **0116 236 4325**
Fax: (00 44) **0116 234 0205**

Other titles in the
Linford Romance Library:

SAVING ALICE

Gina Hollands

Naomi Graham is the best family lawyer in the country. But beneath her professional demeanour lies a broken heart. When the man who caused that heartache — billionaire ex-husband Toren Stirling — returns to her life after a ten-year absence, Naomi doesn't want to know. Their painful struggle to start a family tore their relationship apart, so when Toren reveals that he has a young daughter, Alice, it comes as a shocking blow. Not only that, but he's now fighting a custody battle — and needs Naomi's legal expertise to help him win.